THE HOUSEWIFE ASSASSIN'S

GUIDE TO GRACIOUS KILLING

A NOVEL BY

JOSIE BROWN

PUBLISHED BY SIGNAL PRESS BOOKS

SAN FRANCISCO, CA

MAIL@SIGNALEDITORIAL.COM

Library of Congress Cataloging-in-Publication Data is available upon request

Cover Design by Andrew Brown, ClickTwiceDesign.com

Hardcover ISBN: 978-1-942052-25-8

Trade Paperback ISBN: 978-1-942052-11-1

PRAISE FOR JOSIE BROWN'S NOVELS

"This is a super sexy and fun read that you shouldn't miss! A kick ass woman that can literally kick ass as well as cook and clean. Donna gives a whole new meaning to "taking out the trash."

—Mary Jacobs, *Book Hounds Reviews*

"*The Housewife Assassin's Handbook* by Josie Brown is a fun, sexy and intriguing mystery. Donna Stone is a great heroine—housewives can lead all sorts of double lives, but as an assassin? Who would have seen that one coming? It's a fast-paced read, the gadgets are awesome, and I could just picture Donna fighting off Russian gangsters and skinheads all the while having a pie at home cooling on the windowsill. As a housewife myself, this book was a fantastic escape that had me dreaming "if only" the whole way through. The book doesn't take itself too seriously, which makes for the perfect combination of mystery and humour."

—*Curled Up with a Good Book and a Cup of Tea*

"*The Housewife Assassin's Handbook* is a hilarious, laugh-out-loud read. Donna is a fantastic character—practical, witty, and kick-ass tough. There's plenty of action—both in and out of the bedroom... I especially love the housekeeping tips at the start of each chapter—each with its own deadly twist! This book is perfect for relaxing in the bath with after a long day. I can't wait to read the next in the series. Highly Recommended!"

—*CrimeThrillerGirl.com*

"This was an addictive read—gritty but funny at the same time. I ended up reading it in just one evening and couldn't go to sleep until I knew what the outcome would be! It was action-packed and humorous from the start, and that continued throughout, I was pleased to discover that this is the first of a series and look forward to getting my hands on Book Two so I can see where life takes Donna and her family next!"

—*Me, My Books, and I*

"The two halves of Donna's life make sense. As you follow her story, there's no point where you think of her as "Assassin Donna" vs. "Mummy Donna', her attitude to life is even throughout. I really like how well this is done. And as for Jack. I'll have one of those, please?"

—*The Northern Witch's Book Blog*

NOVELS IN THE HOUSEWIFE ASSASSIN SERIES

The Housewife Assassin's Handbook
(Book 1)

The Housewife Assassin's Guide to Gracious Killing
(Book 2)

The Housewife Assassin's Killer Christmas Tips
(Book 3)

The Housewife Assassin's Relationship Survival Guide
(Book 4)

The Housewife Assassin's Vacation to Die For
(Book 5)

The Housewife Assassin's Recipes for Disaster
(Book 6)

The Housewife Assassin's Hollywood Scream Play
(Book 7)

The Housewife Assassin's Deadly Dossier
(The Series Prequel)

The Housewife Assassin's Killer App
(Book 8)

The Housewife Assassin's Hostage Hosting Tips
(Book 9)

The Housewife Assassin's Garden of Deadly Delights
(Book 10)

*The Housewife Assassin's Tips for
Weddings, Weapons, and Warfare*
(Book 11)

The Housewife Assassin's Husband Hunting Hints
(Book 12)

Chapter 1

Breaking Bad Hostessing Habits

Every woman wants to be the perfect hostess and frets over her inadequacies when it comes to the gracious art of entertaining. Pshaw! A little forethought and a few hours of planning make it as easy as cherry pie!

There is, however, one ironclad rule every hostess must follow:

Make all your guests wish they never had to leave.

Especially in a coffin. With a bullet lodged in their heads.

"You're quite a saucy minx!" Prince Harry's ale-slurred come-on can barely be heard over the techno-vibe emanating from a starship-worthy console of the Ivy Lounge rooftop's head-bobbing deejay. "What say you give me a peek as to where your tattoo ends?"

His head is cocked downward, as if it might give him the ex-ray vision he'll need in order to see the rattle on the faux-tatt'ed snake drawn from my belly to nether regions that lay under my thong bikini.

"You're a cheeky sod. I do have a face, you know." I snap my fingers in front of his nose, in order to draw his eyes northward.

I've succeeded, sort of. But come on, already. The diplomacy born and bred into Prince Henry of Wales (a.k.a. Henry Charles Albert David, but better known as Prince Harry) can't beat two millennia of innate urges and four pints of Guinness.

His eyes linger below my neck, albeit above my abdomen.

When, finally, our eyes meet, I lean in and whisper, "You show me yours, and I'll show you mine."

I'm lying, even if he doesn't know it—yet.

His outright laugh is accompanied with a shake of his head, and a tug at the waistline of his briefs. "No tats under these trollies, I'm afraid. Sorry to disappoint."

I finger his briefs longingly and then sigh. "I'm sure you'll make it up to me somehow."

His smile is his vow not to disappoint.

God save the queen...

It's no secret the prince has been stateside with his Royal Air Force unit, learning the latest tricks and treats of the AH-64D Apache helicopter: his vehicle of choice for his upcoming tour of duty in Afghanistan. The soldiers completed their training today.

Tomorrow they head home. To celebrate, the soldiers are here, in San Diego, which is just a couple of hours west of their training base, the Naval Air Facility at El Centro.

Seems some chatter, intercepted by MI6, has led British intelligence to deduce the prince is the latest target of "the Leprechaun," a notorious assassin affiliated with the Irish terrorist cell known as 32CSM. If the Leprechaun succeeds in picking off the spare to the throne, then once again the always-thin strand of peace between Ireland and Great Britain will be ripped to shreds.

If it happens on our side of the pond, the U.S. will have mud on its face, not to mention the bluest of blood on its hands.

So yep, I have to stop the Leprechaun before he gets lucky.

My employer, the freelance black ops agency known in the field as Acme Corporation, paid big bucks to the club owners so I could be up close and personal with the prince. My goal is not to shag, let alone snag, Harry the Hottie. It's to save his adorable hide from a possible assassination attempt.

The prince leans in, close enough to ask in a seductive albeit ale-sodden growl, "Want me to sign your bikini?"

I look down between my breasts. "Oops, forgot my pen. But you seem to be carrying one, in your pants pocket. Or maybe you're just happy to see me."

He's laughing so hard his last gulp of Guinness goes down the wrong way.

"Prince Charming has a one-track mind." Jack Craig's snarl comes in loud and clear through the tiny microphone in my ear. As the team leader for this Acme mission, he's close by, but far enough away no potential assassin can spot him.

Trust me, there is a hitter lurking nearby.

Jack is also my main squeeze, which is why he's growling about my having to play the coquette while under deep cover (in this bikini, I'm talking figuratively if not literally) as one of the nightclub's VIP bottle girls. More specifically, this is one mission he'd wished I hadn't accomplished—become Harry the Hottie's pick-up du jour.

Needless to say, the club's real bottle girls are pea green with envy. They can't figure out how this newbie became Cinderella of this Century.

If I told them my aim and my first-degree black belt status had something to do with it, would they believe me? Probably not. All they see is that I'm just this side of Cougarville, which means Harry is less discriminating than they had hoped.

For once, I'm glad Jack isn't here, in the cordoned-off VIP section. One involuntary muscle flex and prince's all-too-obvious brawny goon squad—three of his Royal Air Force mates—would be on top of Jack, like suds on ale.

At MI6's behest, we've kept the fact he's a target from Harry, for now, anyway. This, I'm sure, is why he feels so cocksure. This mission wouldn't have been so hard if the prince weren't so insistent about partying "like an ordinary surfer bloke," is how he so preciously puts it.

Until now, the natives have been awed as much by his regular dude personality as his title. But just as the deejay ratchets up the hip-hop club mix, six drunken sorority sisters stroll our way. One of the girls, a Princess Catherine lookalike, pierces me with a jealous glare.

I stare back and smile, as if to say, Take the hint. Get lost.

Her eyes shift from me to one of Harry's RAF buds. She waves coyly at him, and he's smitten. Smirking back, he nods her over. She squeals and grabs the hand of one of her girlfriends.

In no time at all, she and her besties have jumped the red velvet rope. They toss themselves onto the prince's entourage, who don't seem to be fighting them off too hard.

In fact, they're snapping their fingers at me with drink orders for their new arm charms.

"Not good." Jack's warning in my ear is just loud enough for me to hear.

"Tell me something I don't know," I mutter back.

"How about this?" Jack is now shouting into my earpiece. "You've lost Prince Harry."

He's right.

The prince seems captivated by a petite, busty blond beauty. Even in heels, she barely reaches his chest. She had pulled him out onto the dance floor for a throbbing sex-drenched hip grinder, Andree Belle's "Go Go Gadget Heart."

The strobe lights and smoke machine make it hard to follow them in the crowd. Then I see them, against one wall. The buxom little tart drapes her arms around his shoulders and hugs him close, as if she'll never let him go.

Apparently, too close. I shove my way through the crowd until I'm close enough to hear Harry's woozy cry. "Blimey, you're no bird! You've got a wanker!"

Before I can pull him away, the prince is pricked on the neck with something his partner has pulled from her cleavage. Harry's groan is loud. I smell smoke, and then the lights go out. But not before the last strobe catches the triumphant look on his partner's face.

"Oh my God, Jack! The woman with Harry—she's—not a she! She's—"

"I know! I saw it, too! The Leprechaun!"

Proof it pays to hit the M.A.C. counter before a night on the town.

And to hang out where the lights are always low.

Everyone is screaming and shoving their way to the exits, leaving me room to follow the Leprechaun, who is dragging Harry in the opposite direction up against a wall.

"It's too dark to see where they went," I shout to Jack. "Does anything show up on the club's security cams?"

"I'm looking now. In the meantime, check the wall for a hidden pocket door. The schematic of this club shows a few of them on every level. I'm sure the Leprechaun had his exit scoped out in advance."

While Jack scans the feeds from the security cameras, I skim the walls with my hands. Finally, I find it: a tiny catch, waist high.

I pull it open it just in time to see the Leprechaun heaving Harry down a long corridor.

He may not be used to running in heels, but I am. If only I wasn't running in a bikini, too.

"Too many wobbly bits," I mutter under my breath.

It's inappropriate for Jack to be laughing now, but he can't help it. "Just two. And they're a sight to behold. Prince Charming will be upset he slept through it."

The thought of Harry in the French-manicured hands of an assassin who can start the United Kingdom and Ireland down another bloody path of un-neighborly relations has me picking up my pace. Unlike the Leprechaun, I'm smart enough to ditch my high heels. But I'm still not fast enough to reach them before the Leprechaun rolls him into the backseat of a dark BMW and screeches off.

I can hear Jack slapping the wall with his fist. "Aw, damn! We lost them!"

"Nope, I slipped a GPS tracker in the prince's trollies."

"You did what... in his—what?"

"Oh, don't worry, I didn't peek. I'll meet you around the corner."

What's a little white lie between fake husband and wife?

Before he can say another word, I snap off my earpiece and run down the block.

The naval base's commanding officer is cussing up a storm, something about blue-blooded playboy flyboys and horny co-eds.

When, finally, all the steam is out of him, Jack says in the calmest voice possible, "It looks as if they're headed for Mexico, and they've got the jump on us. They're changing vehicles every ten or so miles, which indicates they don't know about the tracker. Not yet, anyway. We can catch them in a 64D, sir."

Before the CO can let loose with yet another tsunami of swear words, I hand him my cell phone. His nods and mutters, indicating he's heard Acme's client—also his boss—loud and clear:

Put whatever we need at our disposal.

We grab Charlie Harcourt-Smythe (he's the soberest of the RAF pilots) and head to the airstrip. Because of the sensitivity of the mission, we'll keep it to that: no FBI, no CIA, and certainly no local law enforcement. The prince has had enough photo ops for one visit.

I've traded in my bikini for a snug wind-resistant flight suit. He never did sign my bikini. Maybe later. If it's not too late already.

Charlie has the Lynx AH.7 pacing the Leprechaun's ride: a sixteen-wheel big rig, barreling down Mexico's Baja Highway. Our guess is he's rendezvousing with some submarine along the coast that will take Harry to an undisclosed location, where he will be tortured on camera as he begs for his life.

From what I've seen of the prince, he'll die before he gives in. He may be royal, but he's no softie.

At that point, he'll lose his life anyway in some macabre fashion, which will have Great Britain's stiff upper lip curling into a retaliatory snarl.

We can't let any of this happen.

Our plan to stop this scenario is simple enough: Jack and I will rappel down from the helicopter onto the truck's bed. Then we'll break into the back and grab Harry, at which point the three of us will be hauled back up into the helicopter.

Our audio surveillance bug, which was shot onto the truck's cab with a mounting magnet, is a real eye-opener in one respect: the Leprechaun has a pretty decent falsetto.

"That little wanker listens to Fiona Apple? Figures." Charlie shakes his head in disgust.

I shrug. "So she's an acquired taste. Could have been worse. Frankly, I was expecting Miley Cyrus."

"More to the point, he's wearing ear buds, so he can't hear us." Jack smiles. "Let's get this show on the road."

My rappelling cord, connected to another mounting magnet, hits its target: the roof of the truck's bed, toward the back. Jack gives me the high sign and I scramble down the rope: not an easy feat, considering the damn thing and the helicopter are moving in tandem, at almost seventy miles per hour. When I land, only my tether saves me from bouncing backward on my ass and toppling off.

Like a crab, I claw and scurry toward the back door. I'm positioned over it when I hear a loud thud behind me. Jack's landing was just as hard as mine. At the speed the truck is going, he'll roll off and take me with him.

Instead, I grab hold of him, as if I'll never let him go.

I won't. Ever.

He murmurs in my ear, "No, that's not a bazooka in my pocket. I'm just happy to see you."

I frown. "Aw, damn. Does this mean you forgot the bazooka?"

Suddenly the truck is zigging and zagging all over the road.

"Bollocks, the tiny bastard knows I'm up here, and that I'm following him." Charlie's voice crackles through our earpieces. "But I don't think he's onto the fact you're on board, so make it quick, lovebirds."

Jack crawls over the side and slams against the doors as he positions the bolt cutter over the lock, and slices through it. He holds onto one door, but lets the other fling open.

We rush inside. Harry is on the floor, trussed up with plastic handcuffs. At least he's alive.

There's a hood over his head. When I pull it off, I see he's bruised badly. Warily, he opens one eye. At the same time, he tries to lift his hands, but can't. That's when he notices he's wearing cuffs. His bleary gaze focuses on me first. "Had I known you liked to play rough, I would have brought along a few of my own toys."

"You're a cheeky toff, you are." I use the bolt cutter to free him, and then toss him a gun. "I'd curtsey, but we're under attack, so let's give it a go, shall we?"

As if hearing me, the Leprechaun breaks hard to the right. The three of us are flung forward. The next thing we hear is the deafening rat-tat-tat of a semi-automatic.

"He's shooting at me," Charlie says. "And I'm tethered to the truck. I've got nowhere to go."

The Lynx is a sitting duck, and so are we, unless we make a run for it. If we scatter, at least one of us may have a chance to take out the Leprechaun before he kills us all.

My mind is racing. "Charlie, on the count of three, we'll jump out of the back. The second we do, program the straight up, and fast, on autopilot. Then eject!"

Harry nods slowly. "Brilliant!"

In theory, perhaps.

"Mind the gap!" I yell as we jump onto the asphalt and roll into scrub. Then we scatter over the wide-open plain. A second later, the Lynx jerks the truck skyward. The Leprechaun is flung forward onto the truck's windshield. He is stunned at first, but still game to take a shot at his target. He fumbles around the floor of the cab for his night goggles and his AP4 LR-308. Finding it, he positions it quickly, so that he has the running prince in his sight.

He is just about to pull the trigger when the helicopter loses the tug of war, and is yanked back to Earth. When the shrieking, twirling dervish slams into the forty-ton truck, the explosion tosses off debris in all directions.

The truck's back bumper hurtles toward me, but I duck just in time. It scorches a path in the dry desert bed before skidding onto a low bank of scrub. I'm choking on the acrid smell of a burning bush.

Despite my tears from the smoke, there is enough light from the fireball for me to scan the desert for Jack and Harry. Yes, they too made it safely beyond the carnage.

Like an errant cloud of fog, Charlie's parachute passes over our heads. A moment later, I hear a thud. "Bollocks! Fecking cactus," Charlie cries. "I won't be able to sit on my arse for at least a week."

Charlie's pain is nothing next to what Jack and I will endure when we break the news to Ryan Clancy, our boss at Acme, that we've demolished one of the Navy's sixty-one million-dollar toys.

In fact, if it weren't for Harry, my guess is that Jack and I would be walking back to San Diego, as opposed to grabbing a seat on the second RAF-piloted helicopter sent to retrieve the prince.

Back at the base, the prince hands me a pair of trollies. His parting gift to me is signed, "xxx! Harry," with his distinctive scrawl.

I smile at Harry. "Thanks mate! What can I say? It's bazzin'."

Okay, now we're even.

CHAPTER 2

THE ART OF GRACIOUS LYING

The ideal hostess has one mission: to make her guests feel as comfortable as possible, at all times. Sometimes this means lying to them.

Should such a time come, little white lies must flow trippingly off the tongue. For example, telling a zaftig friend "You look marvelous, dahling! That floral muumuu is divine..." will certainly thrill her to no end.

However, a greater test is your ability to smile sweetly as you slash the jugular of any thug who has the nerve to crash your soirée as you whisper, "This won't hurt a bit..."

When my children are mad at me, they pout. All it takes is a dozen homemade cupcakes to get back in their good graces.

My hope is that this will also work on my boss, Ryan.

Testing this theory, I place a plate of red velvet cupcakes on his desk, but the scowl stays on his face even as he mutters, "How many of these would we have to sell to recoup the cost of that Apache?"

"Considering the cupcake craze is still going gangbusters in the fly-over states, maybe not as many as you'd think. In fact, if we decorate the icing with tiny pink hearts—"

He lets loose with the sort of groan you hear when a guy watches his favorite team lose the Super Bowl.

Nope, more like what you'd hear from a man who got called on the carpet by POTUS.

"Donna, Donna, Donna. What am I going to do with you?" He holds his head, as if the decision is a painful one.

It could be—for me. Spooklandia urban legend has it that Ryan once ran the CIA's notorious travel agency. You know the one: it specializes in extraordinary renditions, better known as one-way tickets to hell.

Not the best way to see the world.

Its version of Business Class is strapping the passenger, naked, to a hard metal chair and dunking him upside down into a bucket, then threatening to toss him out the door.

The first forty thousand feet are a doozy.

"Sir, surely you can imagine our goal wasn't to crash the copter. And the Cousins have to be satisfied with the mission. We exterminated the Leprechaun while keeping the prince alive."

"They are. Unfortunately, they aren't our client, who must now explain to a committee of media-hungry senators why the prince was joyriding in one of the Navy's precious helicopters before it crash-landed beside a Mexican resort. You're lucky the prince corroborates your story, and luckier still that he's taking the fall."

It's true. The prince is claiming he crashed the Apache.

But the powers that be aren't impressed," Ryan continues. "It would've helped had he not given his testimony via webcam while soaking in a hot tub with five co-eds. Of course, now our client wants assurances you won't be a liability on any future missions."

"I can vouch for Donna, sir." Jack's flippant tone makes me flinch.

"Don't be a smart-ass, Jack. Both of you would've been burned by now, if he hadn't lied to save you." He shakes his head as he sighs. "Well, you can redeem yourself on your next assignment. Another dignitary is being threatened with assassination on American soil."

Great. I pray this one isn't another party animal. "Who is it?"

Ryan tosses a dossier across his broad, slick desk. "The newly elected Russian president, Alexei Asimov."

Jack frowns. "Another one of Putin's puppets."

The dead cold eyes in the photo staring up at me send a chill up my spine. "Wait... isn't he the one they call 'the Grim Reaper of the Ukraine?'"

Ryan nods. "The one and only. We're already hearing chatter about a Ukrainian rebel marksman embedded stateside. And another thread Acme ComInt is following places both Chechen and Russian dissident cells here as well. "

I shake my head in disgust. "Why must we protect the bad guys, too?"

Ryan shrugs. "He's a statesman now. And as long as our country acknowledges him as such, we do, too."

"Is this to be a whirlwind tour of the country? Those are always fun." Ryan knows I'm being sarcastic. I have three kids between the ages of twelve and five. To ensure their lives go on normally, I'll have to line up my Aunt Phyllis.

That's easy. The hard part is putting up with the cattiness that comes with bowing out of carpool. Aunt Phyllis is no help there. Her lead foot on her Volkswagen Beetle is notorious. The Hilldale Police Department is on full alert whenever she's in town, Chechen and Ukrainian assassins be damned.

"Nope," Ryan responds. "In exactly five days, he'll be flying directly into Orange County, specifically for three days of pomp and circumstance, followed by a two-day nuclear disarmament summit. He, POTUS, and twenty-two other heads of state are being hosted by billionaire Jonah Stanford Breck IV in his retreat in your neck of the woods, Hilldale."

When Breck was building Lion's Lair, his posh compound, some of our neighbors had a tizzy fit. What right had he to build an eighty-six-room mansion on the peak of the hill overlooking our quaint little town?

Building his private Getty-worthy museum in the town was the olive branch proffered to, and accepted by, those who were the most upset: the Hilldale Women's Club.

And lucky me, I carpool with the coven running it: Penelope Bing, Tiffy Swift, and Hayley Coxhead.

"The museum is nice, but as for that monstrosity on the hill— well, someone has to say it. There goes the neighborhood," Penelope had muttered.

That doesn't stop her from inviting the Brecks to every social function in town.

They've ignored each invitation, and every one of us, too.

Jack lets loose with a derisive chuckle. "That's a hoot! The richest man in the world, who's made his fortune on military contracts, has turned over a new leaf?"

Ryan shrugs. "Something like that. He's got a new young wife, and a five-year-old daughter. Since his latest marriage, his corporation has sold its arms manufacturing subsidiary. Breck Global Industries now invests only in green technology start-ups, with a focus on sustainable energy and agriculture. To prove it works, he's developed several luxury resorts throughout the world, which rely specifically on eco-friendly energy sources. Fortune has nicknamed him 'the Jolly Green Giant.'"

I'm examining another photo in the dossier: that of Breck and his wife. He's square-jawed, just gray enough at the temples, and his mouth is set in a knowing smirk. Jolly indeed. Babette is a comely blonde in Carolina Herrera. Their daughter, Janie, is a miniature version of her, pearls and all. Babette is his third wife. From the sad look in her eyes, she may not be the last.

Ryan tosses Jack an official-looking badge. "Several financial and media bigwigs have also been invited. Peace isn't a cheap endeavor. Someone has to invest in it, and to get the rest of us to believe they mean it. Acme recently arranged for you—that is, 'Carl'—to accept a partnership in one of the Swiss investment firms invited to this powwow. In the past, the bank has made very substantial investments in Breck Global Industries. As the bank's sole stateside officer, 'Carl' has a ticket to this shindig."

"What's my cover?" I ask.

"You're to become Babette's closest friend in the neighborhood. Your daughters are the same age. Start by setting up a playdate. While this cover won't exactly give you day-to-day access to Lion's Lair, you'll be Jack's plus-one to the reception welcoming Asimov. That would be the prime time for a hit. And if you snuggle up to Babette right, you may have other opportunities to cover Jack, should the need come up."

I can't believe my ears. "What makes you think she wants a new BFF?"

"She's lonely. Breck keeps her on a very short leash."

Jack smiles. "I can see why."

Ryan's slight grin tells me he does, too. "And besides, with the boatload of political dignitaries in town, Breck will be too busy to pay a lot of attention to her."

"Won't the other guests be bringing their wives along for this junket?" I ask.

Ryan shakes his head. "I doubt it. If anything, they'll be relying on Breck to provide any 'diversions' needed. He's a notorious womanizer."

I glance down at the photo of Babette. No wonder she looks so sad.

He points to the pit of humanity beyond his office's glass wall. Case officers are babbling into headsets to deep-cover assets. The eyes on the surveillance operatives dart from webcam to webcam, following targets and warning field agents of any imminent danger.

"Acme already has your team in play," Ryan continues. "Your ComInt will be handled by Emma Honeycutt. If it's okay with you, Donna, we'll have her work out that bonus room you have over that garage."

Jack smiles. "Ah, perfect! The return of the Swedish exchange student, 'Inga Larsson.' I guess Emma's not too happy about going blond one more time, and she fakes a lousy Swedish accent. Ryan, can you ask her to work on that?"

Ryan shakes his head. "Ha! Not on your life. But be my guest."

Just beyond Ryan's glass wall, Emma sits at her desk. She's trying on a long, ash-blond wig over her jet-black punk cut. Jack gives Emma a thumbs-up. She returns his greeting with a middle-finger salute.

Some things never change.

"Because of the tight security mandated by the participating heads of state, everyone attending will be in lock-down mode inside Lion's Lair," Ryan explains. "We've got Arnie Locklear, in tech ops, placed with the florist who will be providing the bouquets in all rooms throughout the estate. That way Arnie can plant bugs where we need them, and monitor them as well. We'll also tap into Breck's security feed, in case we need to divert the guards from seeing you at work. Arnie is working on cracking it now, but the feed is buried pretty deep. In fact, we've yet to learn who is managing security for the event."

Jack nods. "How will we handle any necessary drops?"

"Abu Nagashahi will still be your cutout. He's putting the ice cream truck on hiatus during the summit, so that he can moonlight as the Breck's dog whisperer. That puts him inside the estate, pretty much whenever we need him there. Janie has a Jack Russell that goes by the name of Eddie. Unfortunately, Eddie pees all over the place. If this habit can't be broken during the summit, Breck is threatening to give the dog away."

Well, that certainly has my attention, and not just because I know every kid in Hilldale—including my own—relies on Abu for their mid-afternoon sugar fix. "But Abu hates dogs!"

"For this mission, he's getting over his aversion. We've made sure he came highly recommended from the Brecks' dog trainer."

Jack laughed. "Between handling us and saving Eddie, Abu will have his hands full."

"He'll have some help from Arnie. He's got a few new toys up his sleeve for both of you. He'll debrief you on them tomorrow. "

Through Ryan's glass wall, I spot Arnie at his desk, fiddling with a dog collar. Just then, Emma walks by. Arnie can't help but stop and admire the view. Unfortunately, he doesn't notice that the collar is smoking until it burns his hand, at which point he mouths Damn! Damn! as he drops it to the floor and stomps out the flames. There is no hope this particular gadget is being prepped in time for Abu. In the meantime, I wonder if Emma will ever catch onto the fact he's got a crush on her.

"Jack, now that you have a place at the table, try not to break anything while you're there." He's speaking to both of us, really.

I smile innocently. "If Breck doesn't own a helicopter, I'd say it's doable."

"Are you kidding?" Ryan raises a brow. "He owns a fleet of them. He builds them, remember?"

"Oops! My bad."

"I'm not kidding, Donna. No one but us knows how close the prince came to being the cause of a retaliatory action. If the Ukrainians or Chechens have their way, President Asimov may not be so lucky. Just make sure World War III doesn't happen on your watch."

To prove I'm duly chastised, I nod and keep my mouth shut. Ryan is in no mood for backtalk.

I have kids. I get tired of it, too.

As we turn to leave, I reach for the plate of cupcakes, but Ryan slides it just out of reach.

"Take the dossier. Leave the cupcakes."

It's nice to know I've been forgiven.

My mother was right. The way to a man's heart is through his stomach.

As Jack and I walk toward the car, I toss him the keys to the SUV. "You don't mind picking up the kids, do you? If I'm going to play bestie to a fashionista, I need to do a little shopping."

"Can't it wait? We've got an hour before school lets out. Seeing Harry with his hot tub harem made me realize we rarely take advantage of our own double Jacuzzi tub. What's the use of owning one if we never use it together? You know there's nothing I'd love more than a little afternoon delight. But duty before pleasure. Story of our life, right?"

"Do you mind picking up Trisha from her ballet class? And on the way there, can you drop Mary at her piano teacher's house? Jeff has my permission to hang with Cheever Bing until dinner time."

"I'm getting used to this new Wednesday drill." The tone of Jack's voice is nonchalant, but his smile has faded. His eyes, usually the hue of fresh evergreen, have deepened, too. "I've done it, what, every week this month, am I right?"

"Oh, have you? I hadn't realized." I feel my cheeks flush with guilt.

He shrugs. "No hassle. I love hanging with the kids. You know that."

They love him, too. He is the only father they know. To them—and to the rest of the world, he has lived up to his alias, 'Carl Stone.' The real Carl—the one I loved, lost, avenged heartily, then discovered how he deceived me heartlessly and cruelly—is long gone.

It's finally time to bury him.

"Sure, whatever. I'm sure you'll make it up to me, somehow." He puts his arms around my waist and draws me close to him. His kiss is firm and filled with longing.

I can't help but melt into it. But his loving gaze breaks my heart.

He is an infinite quantum of solace to a woman whose life is pitted with deceit, death and revenge. I guess that's why he doesn't ask what I've been doing on Wednesday afternoons.

Trust me I want to tell him...

But I can't. Instead, I touch his cheek gently with the back of my hand. "Ha! The other moms will be thrilled to have you there. The ballet master, Dimitri Yerkov, is more Nureyev than Baryshnikov. They'll appreciate your male energy."

And let's face it. Jack Craig is primo beefcake.

Best yet, he's all mine.

My kiss good-bye—long, deep, and filled with desire—seals my vows: to him, and to myself.

As soon as I break the vow I made to Carl.

"You still love him, don't you?"

I gasp as I turn to face the man who probes me so deeply. His words cut me deeper than any knife.

My God, I'm in such pain! Does he see it? Why doesn't he care?

But he does. I know this.

Otherwise, we wouldn't be here, like this, together again.

No one knows where I am. The thought of this frees me to be myself in this small, dark room. For the past six Wednesdays, it has been my sanctuary, and he has been my release.

So, why does he want to hurt me now?

To prove the shackles that have bound me for too long can no longer keep me down, I spit out the declaration he has been waiting so patiently to hear these past few weeks:

"No! I don't love him. I can't! Not after what he's done to me."

"Then you know what you have to do, don't you?"

I wince at the question. It smarts worse than any whip, but I'm not defeated. I'm not broken. I'm no longer submissive to my greatest fear:

That, once again, the real Carl Stone will ruin my life.

"Yes, I know what I must do." I'm surprised at how calm my voice sounds.

My inquisitor's lips rise in the slightest of smiles. "Excellent, Donna. And when will you do it?"

During our other covert sessions, whenever I've risen from his black leather chaise, I've ached from the beating I've taken. The memories we fear most do us the most harm. They smack, pummel, and flog us for life.

Today, though, I feel no pain. Instead, I'm as light as a cloud.

"Tomorrow," I answer him. "Tomorrow, I file for divorce from Carl."

My psychiatrist, Dr. Hartley, rises to shake my hand. "You've made excellent progress, Donna—and in such a short amount of time! Some women are unwilling to recognize a husband's desertion as an opportunity to put their lives on a new, better path. They cling to the thought he'll return to them, and that life will go on the way it had before he left. Or they take the blame and punish themselves by staying in an emotional abyss from which they never move on. But not you. With your children, a thriving career and your new relationship, you realize you've got all the ammo you need to annihilate the emotional pull Carl still holds over you."

Ammo. Yep, I've got plenty of that.

But so does Carl.

I have the bullet scar to prove it.

It should be interesting to see how Carl responds to being served divorce papers.

"Donna, in your mind, he's already dead. This is the way it has to be."

"He was dead, Doc. If only he'd stayed that way."

"No, no, no! Repeat after me. 'My ex is dead.'"

I do, three times. If only saying so made it come to pass.

Hearing me say it out loud puts smile on his lips, if not mine. That's okay. My job has taught me how to fake it. "Great session, Doctor Bob! I can tell it was as good for you as it was for me."

My impulsive hug leaves him blushing. Gee, I guess it really was.

CHAPTER 3

WELCOMING NEW NEIGHBORS

Welcoming a new couple into the neighborhood is a wonderful thing to do! A great leave-behind: personalized gifts, in a beautiful keepsake basket you've woven yourself. Consider filling it with fresh flowers and herbs from your garden, a jar of homemade preserves, and perhaps a cake or pie.

Alas, should these newcomers wear out their welcome sooner than you'd hoped, the improvised explosive device you woven into the base of the basket will make the right impression: say, a gigantic hole in the middle of their lot, where their house once stood.

By the time I get home from Dr. Hartley and dress shopping, Jack and the children have already set the table. The homemade vegetable lasagna I left in the fridge for tonight's dinner is bubbling in the oven.

Mary lifts one of my dresses out of its bag for a quick peek, then grimaces. "Dad said you went out to get a party dress. Seriously, this is it?"

Now it's my turn to frown. "What's that supposed to mean?"

She shrugs. "It looks like something my political science teacher would wear."

"Your teacher must have great taste. It's elegant and flattering—"

"And booooring." Mary wrinkles her nose. "Mom, you're hot! You've got it, so why not flaunt it? Especially around totalitarian dictators. Show them what they're missing by suppressing free speech."

I snatch it out of her hand. "I thought I was 'flaunting it.' And by the way, I commend your poli-sci teacher on your knowledge of Asimov."

"Yeah, she sure knows her stuff. In fact, she turned us on to the fact he's sentenced a Russian punk rock group, Pink Taco, to two years in a Siberian prison because they parodied him in a protest song. Our class has started an online petition drive. Our goal is 100,000 signatures from kids all over the country. We're already up to eighty thou—"

"Mommy," Trisha interrupts with a happy squeal, "Daddy and I made new friends! And she's got a pony! She says I can ride it, too. Can we go over to see it tomorrow? Please? Pleasepleasepleasepleaseplease—"

I drop my dress bag as she leaps into my arms and smothers me with kisses.

This is what I live for.

I've killed for the joy I get from my family. No doubt, I'll do so again.

"Yes, of course we'll visit her. What is your new friend's name?"

"Janie." Trisha nods hard with satisfaction. "And her mother's name is Babette. But she told Daddy he could call her 'Anytime.' Isn't that a silly nickname?"

"I'll say." I look around for Jack and find him slumped on the couch next to Jeff. Their keyboards are dueling for health orbs and skill runes in Diablo III. "How about you, dear? Can you imagine calling your new friend, Babette, 'Anytime'?"

"It's just an expression. You know, like, 'have a nice day.'" Jack shrugs, but he doesn't glance over. He's too competitive for that.

Or else he knows better than to face me when I'm jealous.

What the hell is that supposed to mean?

I'll find out later.

In the meantime, I take the lasagna out of the oven and wait until it's cooled a bit before doling it out onto the children's plates and my own, cutting pieces from the sides. Then I slice Jack's wedge from the middle of the casserole, which is still steaming.

You'd think he would have noticed before he bites into it, but no. "Ouch! What the hell, Donna?" In one gulp, he downs all the water in his glass as he glares over at me.

"Sorry. But you know that old expression, 'Cool it or you may get burned.'"

After dinner, I make two pies: one is for us. I'll take the other one over to our newest neighbors, Janie, Babette and Jonah Breck.

Jack eyes them cooling on the counter, but shakes his head when I invite him to take a slice.

"No thanks. It's a lose-lose proposition. If I don't burn my tongue again, I might choose the one with the arsenic."

Good point. Smart man.

He waits until after the kids have cleared the table and are in their bedrooms doing their homework to set things straight. "I didn't know Babette Breck had enrolled their little brat in Trisha's ballet class. It gave me the perfect chance for an introduction, so I took it."

"Then do you care to explain how 'Nice to meet you' becomes 'Call me anytime?'"

"Her exact words were 'Call me anytime about a playdate.'"

My cheeks flare with shame. "I'm sorry. I guess I... well, you know..."

"No, not really. I can't imagine what you were thinking." Jack leans against the wall, his arms crossed. "Feel free to explain. Take your time. It's the highlight of a day in which I've been yelled at by my boss, burned my tongue, and have been hit upon by three very horny housewives while their flat-footed kids twirl around a dance floor—none of whom, I might add, go by the name of Babette." He shakes his head warily. "That woman's as frigid as an ice cube. I waited until she let loose with her last name to mention I'd been invited to the summit. Then she clammed up again. She finally warmed up when Trisha whispered into Janie's ear that she needn't be afraid of Mr. Twinkletoes' Russian rants. In fact, Ryan is beside himself that Trisha's invited over there tomorrow afternoon. He's upset that Acme hasn't been able to locate the security feed. Dropping Trisha off at her playdate will give you the opportunity to scope out the place."

"Me? What, you don't want to go instead?"

Jack's look says it all. I'm being foolish about Babette.

He's right. What's wrong with me?

That's a stupid question. After six weeks of Wednesdays with Dr. Bob, isn't it obvious? I'm jealous. And insecure. Basically, I have trust issues.

Tears roll down my cheeks. "I'm sorry, Jack. Sometimes I'm too stupid for words."

"No, Donna, you're human. Besides, if you didn't care, I'd be asking for a transfer." Jack shakes his head sadly. "Let me ask you, how many times have you played the honeypot on an op?"

I can't help but snort at that question. "When have I not? Okay, say, eighty-five, maybe ninety percent of them."

"Including the ones we've been on together, am I correct?"

My nod is grudging at best. "It's part of the job. And... you've accepted it."

"Yes, I've accepted it. Do you think it's been easy for me?"

I know it hasn't, not since our very first mission together. Jack's assignment—to move in with me and the children and pretend to be my deceased husband, Carl, whom, it turned out, had left the SEALS to become a hard man—an assassin—for Acme.

His "reappearance" (really, Jack's impersonation) provoked the world's most notorious terrorist cell, the Quorum, to come knocking on our door. Apparently, Carl had taken something the Quorum desperately wants. But whatever it is, it has yet to be found.

Unlike Carl, who showed up alive and well.

Turns out, he was a double agent, and one of the Quorum's top assassins.

But Carl's misplaced this item everyone's looking for. I can't imagine what it was, but here's hoping I find it before he does.

Sheesh! After being married to a guy for thirteen years, you'd think I'd have realized something was wrong, am I right? I swear it's true: love is blind.

It blinded me a second time: When Carl resurfaced, he tried to convince me it was Jack who was the double agent. I believed him because I was grateful for his miraculous return from the grave, doubled with the guilt I felt at allowing Jack to replace him: as a father, a husband and a lover.

I believed Carl because I missed his touch so badly.

I wanted to believe him, body and soul.

Boy, was I wrong. Fool me once, shame on you. Fool me twice, take a bullet.

Carl did. Unfortunately, he still got away.

Hopefully, he'll stay away, forever. In any regard, I'm divorcing him. Maybe then, he'll take the broad hint that he blew it. If he doesn't, I'd advise him to watch his back.

Divorces are sooo messy.

So is working with the man you love. I've heard Jack swear into my earpiece as other men touch me. Once, he beat a target within an inch of his life, all because the guy manhandled me too roughly for Jack's taste.

You can only imagine how I crushed Jack's heart when I believed Carl over him.

No, I don't like playing the honeypot. But if I'm to be honest, I have to admit I love the way it stokes Jack's passion for me. No doubt about it: being desired makes you even more desirable to the one who loves you most.

Like now. Forget pie. Jack is what I crave.

My kiss tells him so. "Okay I get it," I murmur into his ear. "I owe you an apology."

"Or something."

I love his naughty smile. And the way his lips know mine so well. Not to mention my neck... my breasts...

One by one, his long, strong fingers nudge open each button on my sweater—

"Mom!" Jeff yells from the top of the steps. "We've finished our homework! Now can we have some pie?"

With a sigh, Jack drops his head onto my breasts. But just for a moment. Our fingers collide as we fumble with my sweater buttons. When I'm sure I'm primly attired again, I call up to the kids to come and get it.

To prove to Jack he can count on my love and devotion anytime, I cut him a humongous piece of pie, and top it with a large dollop of ice cream.

That should keep his tongue in tiptop shape, for later.

Trisha giggles through a mouthful of apple rhubarb. "Mommy got her buttons all wrong! How silly is that?"

I run upstairs before Jeff and Mary figure out what she's talking about.

"How sweet! A pie!" Despite the delight in her tone, Babette stares down at my offering as if she's already gotten a memo from Jack about my extraordinary baking skills.

"Apple rhubarb," I inform her with a smile. "The crust is from a recipe handed down from my great-grandmother."

Not really. I found it on Martha Stewart's website. I'm guessing Babette knows Martha personally and has tasted pie made from the entertainment maven's very own hands, since both of them own quaint little abodes in Westchester County, New York.

In fact, the Brecks own homes practically everywhere—New York, London, Paris, Lake Como, Rio de Janeiro, Gstaad, St. Tropez, St. Barts, St. Petersburg (Russia, not Florida)—all of which are fully staffed.

Babette hands my pie over to the butler, then ushers us through a reception hall, to one of the estate's living rooms. I kid you not, it's got to be the size of the Hall of Mirrors in Versailles. In fact...

"Excuse me, this may be a silly question, but... well, is this room—?"

Babette's sigh is long and practiced. "Yes. An exact replica. Trust me, it was Jonah's idea, not mine."

She bends down slightly so that the slight heat of her tepid smile warms at least one of us: Trisha takes it as her cue to give a proper curtsey.

Note to self: no more episodes of Downton Abbey for my youngest. Maybe it's time I read her Les Misérables. Or at least take her to see the musical.

The sounds of whinnying and laughter come from the vast velvety lawn that stretches beyond the French doors and onto infinity. At the sight of Janie on a dappled Shetland pony—in jodhpurs, riding helmet and show coat, no less—Trisha's manners take flight, and so does she, right out an open door.

I shake my head in mock embarrassment. "Please forgive Trisha. She's very excited about meeting Janie's pony."

"Not at all. Janie took to Trisha instantly. It's a blessing, since we're always on the move. Normally, she finds it so hard to make friends." With this admission, sadness clouds her eyes.

Our children give us a reason to look away. By now, Janie's trainer has helped her off the pony. Eddie the dog, leashed and detained a hundred feet away by Acme's undercover agent, Abu, jerks and jumps in frenzied frustration. Janie and Trisha hug each óther, then Janie takes Trisha's hand and places it gently, palm up on the pony's nose. When the pony snorts and shakes its head, both girls giggle and run off to the stable just beyond the house.

Eddie yanks free from Abu and runs after them. Thank goodness Abu's curses are muttered in some ancient Punjabi dialect. I'll bet, right about now, he wishes he were wrangling with some eight-year-old over the price of an ice cream sandwich instead of chasing Eddie around the yard.

"Feel free to leave Trisha for the afternoon," Babette offers. "In fact, may she join us for dinner and perhaps a sleepover? She and Janie can eat in the playroom with Antoinette, Janie's au pair. She'll bathe them, and Trisha can borrow a pair of her pajamas. Janie is bored to death at our formal dinner parties. I'll let you in on a little secret: I am, too."

This time Babette's smile seems genuine.

I wish I could feel sorry for her, but I'm sure living in a miniature version of Versailles compensates for a lot.

Babette stops short, as if something has just crossed her mind. "Your husband mentioned he'll be attending Jonah's disarmament summit. Perhaps you and Carl would like to join us for dinner tonight as well?"

It's my turn to fake a smile. "That would be nice. We look forward to it."

Ryan is going to break out in a happy dance when he hears Jack and I will be in Lion's Lair sooner than expected. This gives Acme another shot at finding the source for Breck's security feed before the summit. Thus far, the only thing Arnie has been able to determine via the estate's architectural plans is that the hub is

36

somewhere in the vicinity of Breck's office wing, which has been off-limits to Arnie, since Breck doesn't like flowers in that room.

"It will be an intimate group," Babette continues. "Just some of Jonah's key executive staff, and a couple of German investment bankers who've arrived in advance of the event." Her brow rises with the curl of her lip. "Acclimating to the time difference is always a marvelous excuse to come stateside earlier than needed. Not that I blame them. Orange County is a delight this time of year compared to Hamburg."

An early arrival gives them time for reconnaissance, too.

I'm sure Acme already has the summit's attendee roster in hand, but this information comes in handy, in case one these men has something to do with the assassination attempt.

"Oh dear, how time flies! I have a meeting with the chef to go over the menu, so if you'll excuse me," she says as she walks me to the door. "By the way, the dress code is black tie. Jonah prefers it that way." As breathy as her air kiss is her murmur. "I'm sure you have something that will please him."

Before I have a chance to reply, she shuts the door.

What the hell is that supposed to mean?

CHAPTER 4

HOW TO CHOOSE A PARTY DRESS

When you're a guest at someone else's soirée, your first impression should be also be a lasting one—and certainly not because you either overdressed, or underdressed, for the occasion. When in doubt, keep it simple and elegant: black, with pearls.

If the dress code is not in the invitation, take the time to query your host regarding the proper attire.

Note of caution: should your host's recommendation include, say, crotchless panties, a naughty schoolgirl plaid skirt, brocade ankle restraints and a head harness with a muzzle gag, be sure to bring along something you'll know he deserves, for getting on your bad side.

A cement overcoat will do nicely.

"Go with the backless one. You've got the shoulders to carry it off."

I turn around to see who's offering an opinion on my hunt for the right gown to the Breck shindig tonight. My advisor is a man who sits on a settee in a darkened corner of the Bergdorf-Goodman couture suite, just off to the side of the circular bank of mirrors.

While I've been scrutinizing my profile, he's been admiring my shoulders, supposedly. But only now does he lift his eyes— from somewhere far below my shoulders—to meet mine.

From the look of his suit (made to measure for a man whose fit physique would look great in a gunnysack, let alone a fifteen-thousand-dollar charcoal gray Brioni) he has great taste.

He should. He is Jonah Stanford Breck IV, one of the wealthiest men in the world.

Sweetly, I smile at him through the mirror. "You like it better than the blue one?"

His eyes sweep over me, appraisingly. "Much more so. Albeit the blue sets off your... eyes."

I laugh at his ridiculous attempt to avoid the obvious. My eyes are brown. What looks great in the blue dress is my ass.

We both know it.

"Great, then. The blue one's the charm."

"You'll be the belle of the ball."

"Not a ball, really. Just dinner. In fact, I'll be dining at your place, Mr. Breck."

His eyes, gray like his trimmed sideburns, flash suspiciously for a moment before dulling into wariness.

"Your wife, Babette, extended the invitation. My daughter, Trisha, has been playing with Janie all afternoon. I presume Babette felt the diversion would be welcomed."

"Ah! How thoughtful of her. She's right. These business affairs can be deadly without a few petite amusements."

As if on cue, a woman in a flesh-toned, sparkly low-cut gown walks out of one of the dressing rooms and over to Breck. She turns her back toward him, just slightly. "Zip me up, will you, darling?" Her murmur is deep and soft, like velvet.

Slowly, he runs the zipper along the swayed arch of her back then pats her ass, not so much to let her know he is done with her, but as a promise that he isn't.

His eyes stay with her as she makes her way back to the dressing room. Finally, as if remembering I was still in the room, he adds, "She's Babette's personal shopper. Unlike me, after eight years of marriage, my wife finds trekking through stores 'a chore and a bore.' Marilyn is exactly her size and coloring, so these little shopping excursions are win-win for everyone. Beautiful, don't you agree?"

"The woman or the dress?"

He points to my profile in the mirror. "A beautiful woman makes the dress."

I smile my thanks. "Then I presume I've just had a preview of what Babette will be wearing?"

His smile fades. "Don't presume anything. Babette doesn't always agree with my taste."

"A shame. So fetching."

It is his turn to ask, "The woman, or the dress?"

"Since you're paying, you tell me."

He laughs uproariously at that. "I always do. And dearly."

"Speaking of the dear, will she be joining us for dinner?"

His smile hardens into a smirk. "Later. Dessert. I have a voracious appetite, especially for sweet things." His eyes catch mine in the mirror. "Remember, dinner at eight. Sharp."

By the time I leave the dressing room, Jonah Breck and his personal shopper have already checked out.

When I take my dress to the sales clerk, she informs me, "Mr. Breck put it on his tab. He asked me to relay his sincere appreciation for your daughter's hospitality, and he looks forward to returning it, personally."

I guess I can tell Ryan he need not worry whether we'll get close enough to the summit's host. If Breck has his way, we'll be up close and personal.

Or at least, I will.

Oh yeah, Jack should love that.

CHAPTER 5

SUCH GRACIOUS CONDESCENSION

You have an excellent chance to impress new friends when you are a guest in their abode. The food, libations and ambiance was created by your host and hostess for the purpose of impressing you, so do go out of your way to be generous with your compliments! Spare no words in describing your appreciation of their furnishings and décor, as well as the little touches that make their house a home. And certainly, you should never come empty-handed. A bottle of wine will do, or perhaps flowers.

A note of caution: Be sure to eyeball all the exits, both doors and windows. This way, should you somehow insult your host (or, say, rile them into a frenzy) your getaway can be quick.

Having a helicopter standing by is never a bad idea, either.

"What else did he say, other than he wants to get into your pants?" Jack sits at the edge of the bed. Yes, he's dressed for dinner, except that the top button on his tux shirt is open. The ends of his bowtie hang around his unbuttoned collar.

My mascara brush stops mid-stroke. I frown back at Jack through the mirror. "He didn't come out and say that. It was merely implied. And for accuracy's sake, it wasn't my pants he wanted to get into, but my dress."

"Semantics aside, did he mention Asimov?"

I cock a brow. "Asimov was the last thing on his mind, trust me."

Jack grimaces. "No doubt, we can use the fact he's sniffing around you to our advantage. But watch yourself around Breck, Donna. There's a lot about this dude that doesn't add up."

I walked over to him. After fastening the errant button, I loop the strands of his tie into a proper bow. "It's cute that you're jealous."

"I'm not jealous... Okay, yeah, maybe. But that's not what this conversation is about. The stuff Emma is picking up on him leads me to believe the faithful husband, indulgent father and peace facilitator hasn't totally changed his spots."

"You're telling me! I caught him with one of his arm charms."

Jack shrugs. "Why am I not surprised? He's a walking aphrodisiac: wealth and power."

"Tell that to Babette. Nope, scratch that. I'd hate for her to seek solace in the arms of the messenger." That vision has me clenching his bowtie a bit too tight.

He pulls me into his lap. It could be survival instinct, but his passionate kiss tells me otherwise.

Yep, Jack's gag reflexes are working just fine.

Unlike this afternoon when I dropped Trisha on her playdate, tonight the Lion's Lair is a gilded fortress, both figuratively and literally.

Instead of one guard at the gate, there are three armed guards, and a security detail roams the park-like grounds like big, hungry cats on the prowl for dangerous prey. I even spot a few guards in the turrets crowning the estate.

Jack gives a long low whistle. "Man! I can see why they're holding the summit here. Looks like Breck has all the bases covered."

I shrug. "Not if it's an inside job."

He knows I'm right. That's why we've both memorized the dossier of Breck's nearest and dearest friends and associates, several of whom, we presume will be dining with us tonight. Emma also pulled intel on the two German businessmen who came into town early for this shindig. Thus far, they look clean, but you never know.

Sometime during dinner, I'm supposed to excuse myself to check on Trisha and Janie. On the way to the nursery, I'll make a quick detour into Breck's office, where I'll find his computer, and insert a tiny computer thumb drive, hidden in my bracelet. It contains a shadow virus, which will read all of Breck's keystrokes, and relay them back to Arnie. At the same time, it will download all the computer's files. When I return the thumb drive to Arnie, he can search it for the code to the feed.

The whole thing is supposed to take no more than three minutes.

Jack and I smile pretty at the guard who stops our car. Yes, our names are on his manifest, so are photos of us, obviously taken today: mine, when I was ringing the front door with Trisha in hand; and Jack's, as he and Trisha walked out of the ballet studio with Babette and Janie.

"Well, what do you know," I murmur as I freshen my lipstick. "We're being shadowed."

The guard has us sign the manifest, then he scans our thumbs and our eyes.

"I wonder if they did this to Trisha," Jack says, as we drive away toward the front door, where we're met by a valet, who whisks the car off to some point beyond the six-car garage. "When we get back into the SUV, no talk beyond chitchat," Jack warns me.

I nod slightly. Like, me, he knows our car will have been bugged by the time we're ready to go home.

Are we having fun yet?

"Ah, Mrs. Stone, a pleasure." Even as Jonah Breck shakes my hand, his eyes appraise me from head to toe. "So good of you to come. You're a stunning addition to our table."

I can tell he's pleased I wore the dress he not only recommended but paid for, too. Good manners dictate I should've returned the dress with a note that was gracious, but firm in doing so. However, Ryan talked me out of it. "You've got his attention? Great! It means your presence won't seem out of place. Keep playing up to him."

Jack's frown may have been missed by Ryan, but I certainly caught it.

I've no doubt he loves me as much as I love him. All the more reason to divorce Carl: so I—so we—can get on with the rest of our lives.

Babette stands by his side. She shakes my hand first, then Jack's. Does she hold onto it a moment too long?

I've got to quit being so paranoid.

And yes, she's wearing the dress I saw earlier today on Marilyn.

Jack and I are introduced to the others, all of whom I recognize from the dossier. They include Breck's attorney Garrett Conover: too tall, too thin, and with a smile that is too wide to be genuine, apropos for the angel of death who dotted the i's and crossed the t's on all of Breck's arms deals.

Then there's the chief operating officer of Breck Global Industries: Rutherford Collins, Breck's sniveling yes-man who delivered the WMDs under budget and on schedule. How are these guys adjusting to Breck's new mantra, Give peace a chance? It should be interesting to see.

Along with Babette and myself, the other women joining us for dinner are a rod thin and tough-as-steel über-public relations flack with the face of a bulldog named Felicity Tolliver; and Breck's personal assistant, Edwina Doyle. Our intel describes her as just north of thirty, single, efficient, and hailing from Paris. Her picture was kinder to her. In person, she is pale and mousy.

In other words, neither is the type who would tempt Breck.

Considering all he has to lose, I'd say that's a smart move on his part. No need to dip his pen in company ink when there are so many other places to put it... or something.

The dining room isn't one at all, but a library, which is supposed to be "cozy," despite its football-field-length, wall-to-ceiling books, two-story-high ceilings, and a fireplace large enough to hold three men and a little Bentley.

The table is round, which allows for optimum placement of the eight guests between the host and hostess. I'm seated to the right of Breck, and Franz is next to me. On his right is Felicity, with Rutherford beside her. That puts Babette to his right and directly across the table from Breck. Jack sits to Babette's right, and Edwina on the other side of him, with Garrett on her right. Hans is sandwiched between Garrett and Breck.

Franz and Hans, who sit opposite each other, speak perfect English to everyone else, but hold side discussions in their native language. My earrings are embedded with an audio feed that allows Ryan to whisper sweet nothings into my ear. He promises to do so, should the bugs Arnie has planted in the flowers that adorn the table and the rest of the room pick up anything Jack and I should be warned about. It will be interesting to hear the translation between Franz and Hans. Even if their phrases are seemingly innocuous, I wonder if any codes will be detected.

For the most part, the conversation is polite, the service by a phalanx of butlers is attentive to a fault, and the meal is perfect. How can you go wrong with piquillo gazpacho as your first course, followed by a chilled Dungeness crab salad, roasted Pacific Northwest salmon with a vegetable ragout, and lime meringue pie topped with mango and raspberry ice sorbet? And of course, each course served with white and red gold-medal varietals.

In social settings, what is said isn't as important as what you see. Even before the appetizer was served, Edwina had shifted her body away from Garrett, as if to avoid him and to focus on Jack. I can't blame her. The guy gives me the willies, too.

Jack is gracious enough to answer her questions about the community and his role in his investment firm, but he's smart enough to share his remarks and attentions with Babette.

Garrett's placement must be ideal for him, because he's practically fawning over Hans. Even when I compliment her on her dress, Felicity ignores me and does the same to Franz. Once snubbed, twice considering slipping a roofie into her wine glass. What am I, chopped liver?

No. Apparently, I'm presumed to be Breck's playmate du jour.

This is made obvious by the leer and wink he gives me after I try to broach the topic of Great Britain's LIBOR debacle and its affect on American banks. I have to bite my tongue to keep from telling him that it's me, not my breasts, speaking to him.

Right as the main course is served, Jack looks over at me. Feigning concern, he asks, "Donna dear, you promised Trisha you'd bring her teddy bear. Have you given it to her yet?"

"Oh! No...I have it in my purse." I glance over at Babette. "If you don't mind, Babette, I'll just walk it down to the nursery."

Babette nods. With a slight wave, she summons over one of the butlers. "Jamison will show you the way."

Trisha is happy to get a kiss, a hug and her teddy bear, but she makes it clear that she's not ready to go home by putting her arm around her new pal and burrowing under the blanket they share. Nothing like bonding over ice cream in bed while Brave plays on a screen that takes up one whole wall of the nursery.

Ah, the good life.

Jamison has already scurried back to his post, having been assured I can easily find my way back.

I can, but I don't. Instead, I take a detour into Breck's office and go to work.

The room is simple and elegant. Over a credenza is a John Singer Sargent portrait of a young wasp-waisted Victorian beauty. On another wall, a crowd meanders through a Parisian market through the surrealistic eyes of Georges Seurat.

Breck's desk is large, glass, and empty. Where the hell is his computer?

Then I see it: a laptop, on the credenza.

Quickly, I remove a thumb drive from my bracelet and insert it into the computer. While it does its thing, I lean over the desk for a better look at the Sargent...

"Beautiful, isn't she?"

Breck's voice sends a trickle of dread down my spine.

I lift my lips into a smile before turning around. "I saw it first a few years ago, when you loaned it to the Getty. It is one of my favor—"

Before I can finish my sentence, his tongue is down my throat, and his hand is on the lower part of my back. He has me leaning so far back that I'm practically horizontal across the credenza.

Sure, I could bite his tongue until he squeals in pain. And yeah, I can yank his arm out of the socket so that it hangs helplessly at his side. But if I do that before another two minutes is up, I'll blow our mission to hell.

So instead, I try not to gag as he cups me on the ass and grinds into me. I moan as if I like it. In truth, this horizontal boogieman has me pressed up against something sharp. I reach behind to pull it out—

Hmmm, a sterling silver letter opener, engraved with his initials. As he conducts a more thorough incisor exam than I've gotten from my dentist, I try to guess how far his blood would spurt if I follow through on my urge to stab his jugular with it.

Out of the corner of my eye, I notice the thumb drive is blinking. It's my cue to kiss him hard, and grab it fast.

I reach over slowly. Unfortunately, this means I have to inch closer to Breck. He takes it as a cue to fumble with his belt and zipper.

Um.... No. No way in hell—

I whip out the thumb drive. Then, as I push him away, I gasp, "I—I can't do this! I love my husband too much!"

His smile fades. He stares down at me, as if deciding if I'm serious, or just a tease.

In any event, he's still intrigued. I know this because he bruises my lips with a long kiss, then murmurs, "You can. And you will."

He takes my smile as tacit understanding that he's right.

Wrong. I have to force myself to drop the envelope opener, before I do something I'll regret.

He zips up, and then straightens his jacket and tie. "In the meantime, feel free to hang out with Babette during the summit. I want you two to get to know each other well. That way, when you give up your pathetic attempt at propriety, she won't suspect a thing."

Without a backward glance, he walks out the door.

Jeez. Seriously? Whatever happened to "ladies first?"

The man needs a lesson in good manners.

Accompanied by a horsewhip.

By the time we get back to the dining library, the conversation has shifted from the global economy to curiosity about the natives in their natural habitat.

"The town of Hilldale is nothing like we had expected," Franz says to me in his booming voice. "So close to Los Angeles, but seemingly unsullied by all the celebrity glamour, or its big city problems. Your little burg is quite quaint, in an All-American way. It reminds me of that American television program: Leave it to Beaver, ja?"

I nod. "I fell in love with Hilldale the moment I saw it. I'm sure Babette feels the same way."

All eyes sweep toward our hostess, including Breck's.

"In all honesty, I really haven't had time to enjoy it." She toys with her fork. "Lion's Lair was only completed a few months ago. In the meantime, we go where Jonah's business takes us—which, as you can imagine, is all over the world. But now that Janie is at an age where school and friends are becoming important, I wouldn't mind putting down roots in a place that revels in normalcy."

"'Normal'? Is that how Hilldale seems to you, my dear?" Breck's tone sounds sincere, but his eyes give him away. He's mocking her.

Why do I feel as if I'm watching a cat toy with a mouse?

"Well... yes, of course." Babette's cheeks turn rosy with embarrassment. "As Franz points out, it's the all-American dream. Comfortable homes, beautiful tree-lined streets, nice shops, wonderful schools. And our neighbors seem very nice." She glances over at me, but her voice trails off, betraying her attempt at a convincing argument.

"They should be." Franklin sniffed. "We built our museum here. It's put this little hovel of a town on the map."

Jack shrugged. "Consider it money well spent. Think of all the goodwill it bought you. This same estate, built in LA County, would have tripled your tax base, without all the benefits Babette just pointed out. And you're only a half hour from the city, forty minutes from LAX—or more appropriately, in your case, Santa Monica Municipal."

"My point isn't that Hilldale has its upside. It's that even this town has its dirty little secrets." Breck strokes the stem of his port snifter. "Did you know that there are four convicted child molesters in Hilldale? Or that last year alone, there were twenty-eight cases of domestic violence, and three meth houses were raided? Five former porn stars have 'retired' here. I use that word loosely, considering the economy has everyone out there beating the bushes—or something—to make a buck. By the way, two of your neighbors are in the Witness Protection program. And let's not forget the eight guys whose last homes were minimum-security Federal penitentiaries, where they were incarcerated for white collar crimes."

Jack laughs. "You've certainly done your homework, Jonah."

"If I'm truly going to make Hilldale my home, I want to know where all the bodies are buried."

If he were nicer, I'd fill him in on that. As it is, he's got enough reconnaissance to find out on his own.

"You see, my dear, there is no place on earth with the kind of tranquility we crave. All the more reason this summit has to succeed. If we want a perfect society, we have to build it from scratch." Breck sighs. "Suddenly, I've got a voracious appetite for something sweet. I guess you're right about me, Babette. I'm never satisfied."

The dinner ends a little before midnight. Jack and I don't speak on the drive home. Instead, we crank up the car's stereo.

We have no doubt we're being bugged.

When we get to the house, we pull into the garage and close the door behind us.

In a few hours, an Acme tech team will enter the garage through the door leading into it from the backyard and do a thorough sweep for audio and GPS bugs, crushing them in the middle of the street as if a large pothole knocked the damn thing loose.

In fact, Acme will create the pothole.

Our neighbors, whose cars will also hit it, will curse the hole and Town Hall until the damn thing is fixed.

As Breck pointed out, paradise is still a distant dream.

We have a motorcycle parked in the shed out back. While it's still dark and Aunt Phyllis enjoys Stephen Colbert's truthiness, we rev it up and head out for Acme, but we take a circuitous route in case we're being followed.

Since our bike's GPS is on Acme's private satellite surveillance feed, we're informed that we're in the clear, even before we get to Acme headquarters.

Once here, Arnie practically snatches the thumb drive out of my hand. It takes him all of eight minutes to retrieve and crack open the files holding the info on the Breck estate's security feed.

Bottled beer is the way Acme celebrates its ability to shadow all the webcams in every room of Lion's Lair. "Hot shit," Arnie exclaims, "I've got access to the archival footage, too."

"So, open a file. I know, let's see what the swells had for dinner tonight," Emma says impatiently. "I'm guessing it wasn't vegan."

Not to let her down, Arnie clicks open a file with the time stamp of 9:13 p.m. A bathroom that is empty, thank goodness. The nursery shows Trisha and Janie playing with Legos. Two guards, sharing a smoke in an outdoor alcove. A cook in the kitchen, scrubbing a pot.

Yep, every room. Including Breck's office, where my Acme team watch as Breck attacks me on the credenza.

Jack's eyes narrow as he watches. Arnie, Ryan and Emma are smart enough to get the hell out of the room.

I stay to face the music.

"You said nothing happened!" Jack grabs me by the wrist as if he wants to shake some sense into me. "The son of a bitch practically rapes you, and you call that nothing?"

"I stopped it the moment I got the intel we were after, didn't I? Mission accomplished, right?" I yank my wrist out of his hand.

My instinct is to slap him.

No, to cradle his face. To gently wipe away the anger I see there.

Our kisses are deep, sweet and desperate. We know we should stop it, that we should get a hold of ourselves, but we can't. We won't. He's lost in his pain. I'm driven by my desire to have nothing come between us, ever.

Certainly not Jonah Breck.

As if reading my mind, Jack's lips finally part from mine. "I hate the fact that you're so good at what you do."

How do I answer that?

I can't.

Not now, anyway.

Ask me again when I'm a free woman, and we can both walk away from this life, together.

Not that anyone ever does.

But come hell or high water, we will certainly die trying.

Together.

As we leave, I ask Arnie to exchange my break-in with a loop of Breck's empty office. That way, unless someone has replayed it between now and then, I'm in the clear.

And so is Breck, that son of a bitch.

CHAPTER 6

HOW TO MAKE A FORMAL INTRODUCTION

When formally introducing one friend to another, take the hand of the first friend as you ask for the attention of the second, in this manner:

"Lavinia, for the longest time I've been looking forward to introducing you to Hortense Whatshername. She makes the most delicious chocolate Bundt cakes, and is a great fan of Dickens! Hortense, this is my dear friend Lavinia CantStandsYa! She throws the most interesting potluck book salons, which is now reading every Dickens novel, in alphabetical order. I think you two will have a lot in common."

Then pat them both on the back, and step away.

In fact, run as far away as possible, especially if you've planted an IED in Hortense's Bundt cake, since your objective is to be far outside of the debris field.

"Mommy! MOMMY!" Trisha is standing at the front door, screaming at the top of her lungs. "Cheever Bing's mother is at the front door, with those other women you think are silly gooses, too!"

Great. Just great. It's too early in the morning for this—and on a Saturday, no less. Since seven, Jack and I have been glued to our iPads, which now contains the intel Arnie has been extracting all night from Breck's security feed. Jack is memorizing the dossiers on the strategy teams and security details of every head-of-state who will be attending, while Emma, now set up in the room over the garage, debriefs me via phone on the chatter around the deployment of three known assassins. One is Chechen, another is Ukrainian, and the last is a Soviet rogue agent.

Not only am I up to my armpits in Acme intel, assassin sightings, and the quest for a divorce attorney, now I have to deal with Penelope Bing and her momtourage?

Not to mention whatever Jack has in mind for Breck. Copping a feel is going to cost him, big time.

Just like Trisha's "silly gooses" declaration is sure to cost me something with the Bitches of Hilldale.

I have no desire to find out what. "I'll be right there," I holler down the stairwell. Not really. Better to send Jack instead. He'll schmooze, flatter, make promises I can't keep, and walk them out the door.

Damn. The risky part is all those promises. Still, I can't keep Emma hanging on the line, so I wrap my arms around Jack's neck and nuzzle his ear. "Jack, sweetie, how about going down and make up some excuse as to why I can't see them?"

He groans. "You're not serious, are you?"

"They like you! They'll buy anything you're selling."

"Yeah, that's the point. There's nothing I wish to part with. Not to them, anyway."

"Please? Pretty please? With sugar on top?" I make a frownie face. It works for Trisha, so why not for me?

Jack shakes his head and stretches tall, as if that will overcome a night of just three hours of sleep. Then he rummages for a T-shirt, finding one at the foot of the bed, and pulls it on over his drawstring running pants. It's tight around his broad back and his bulging muscles. He hasn't shaved yet, and his five o'clock shadow is prickly.

Aw, hell. If I send him down there, Penelope will never want to leave.

"Mommy!" Trisha's yells, even more frantic now. "They brought a cake! Can I have some?"

Cake? That means Penelope is after something. And when Penelope has her mind set, even Jack won't be able to get rid of her. "Wait, I'll go down instead—"

"What, are you crazy? Penelope brought a cake? I'm outta here!"

"Remember," I hiss at him, "promise her nothing! Nothing!"

Too late. Jack can't hear me because he's already halfway down the stairs.

Oh well. The way he looks, Penelope certainly won't miss me for another ten minutes. I turn back to the phone receiver. "Emma, what were you saying about the Russian assassin?"

"Um... I'll tell you in person. If you've got cake for breakfast, I'm coming right down."

"But I was going to make oatmeal for everyone."

It's no use. She has already clicked off. She can't stand wearing that silly blond Inga wig, but she hates my oatmeal even more.

They all do. Too bad. It's good for them. Heart-healthy, lots of fiber.

Oh, who the heck am I kidding? I better get my ass down there before all the cake is gone.

Coffee has been poured. Apparently, the women have brought a Bundt cake.

By the time I get downstairs, Emma is already digging into a piece. As Inga, her bad Swedish accent allows her to beg off any attempt at conversation.

I get no such reprieve, despite knowing firsthand that nothing these women do or say makes any sense.

Trisha's mouth looks as if she's sporting a chocolate mustache, and Penelope Bing, Tiffy Swift, and Hayley Coxhead are giggling like little school girls. Not at Trisha, but at Jack, who has to bend down as he rummages through the fridge for some crème fraiche to lighten their brews.

Needless to say, no one looks up when I enter. The view is too captivating.

My taxi whistle grabs their attention. "What a nice surprise," I murmur as I air kiss Penelope. "Excuse me for not opening the door for you. We had a late night, and as you can see, we were still in bed." I nod toward Jack, who is cutting a wedge of cake for himself that's the size of New York's infamous Flatiron Building.

Considering he has a size forty-inch chest, thirty-two-inch waist, washboard abs and the ass of a twenty-six-year-old fireman, I'm sure they're wondering where he puts it all.

Wouldn't they like to know.

Tiffy nudges Penelope out of whatever fantasy she's having about Jack. I guess it is show time.

Penelope takes one last, longing glance at him. When she's done, the dewy look in her eyes hardens even before they reach me. Game on. "Donna, darling, this is strictly a social visit. Hayley, Tiffy and I were talking about you just the other day: how it seems that... well, since Nola's sudden move out of the neighborhood, you haven't quite been yourself. We know how close the two of you were, and it pains us to see you so lonely."

What a bitch! Penelope knows quite well that I couldn't stand Nola. For that matter, there wasn't a woman in Hilldale who liked her.

How could they? She was the neighborhood slut.

And unbeknownst to me, until her grisly and untimely death—at the hands of the real Carl—she was an Acme agent under deep cover. Her assignment: to watch over me and my family, should the Quorum somehow coming knocking on my door in search of what Carl left behind.

The Quorum did show up, and with the best Trojan horse it could send in: Carl.

Nola's reconnaissance allowed Acme to pull the ultimate endgame: put Jack in Carl's place. After a five-year disappearance on the day after we moved into the neighborhood, who would know he wasn't my husband?

Me. Yes, I balked at first, but I soon got over it.

He is now the spy who loves me.

Cozying up to Carl cost Nola her life. But before she died, she was able to pass vital intel to Jack, which allowed us to stop Carl and the Quorum from pulling off one of the most horrendous terrorist acts ever conceived.

I realized too late that Nola was really a friend.

I said so, too late. Unfortunately, it was at her funeral, which was attended only by her Acme colleagues.

Acme's cleaning service made it look as if she left town suddenly. The neighborhood gossips (three of whom have brought me this chocolate Bundt cake to die for) thought this may have had something to do with Jack's late night encounters with Nola, which, apparently, were the talk of the town.

Little did they—or I—know, at the time, Nola would soon sacrifice her own life in order to save the whole Los Angeles metro area.

This is why, when Hayley pats my hand and murmurs in mock sympathy, "You must miss her terribly," I must resist the urge to shove her face into what's left of Penelope's Bundt cake.

Instead, I look her right in the eye when I say, "Yes, Hayley, I do."

"Well, we think it's marvelous that you've reached out to some of our new neighbors, in the hope of filling the gap," Penelope declares briskly. "And you, too, Carl."

Jack chokes on his cake. "Um... come again?"

Penelope honors him with an innocent smile. "Seems that Donna is great friends with Babette Breck."

"Tiffy saw you at ballet practice with Trisha, Carl. She noticed you seemed quite chummy with Babette, too." Hayley can't wait to get that out. She gives me a sidelong glance. I'm sure she's hoping for an explosive reaction.

Well, she isn't going to get one. "Oh? I didn't know your son, Logan, takes ballet, Tiffy."

Tiffy blushes. Logan is nine and a bruiser. Her husband, Rex, is a Neanderthal. He would bust a gut if his kid participated in anything but football or wrestling. "Oh... no! Logan wouldn't be caught dead in a ballet studio. I was at the pharmacy when I saw Carl with Babette, and..."

Her voice trails off. We can all figure out why, but I want to rub it in, anyway. "That's odd," I say as innocently as possible, "the pharmacy is four blocks away, on another street. You must have ex-ray vision."

Penelope's fork clatters onto her plate. "The point Tiffy is trying to make is that we find it admirable that you've taken

Babette under your wing." She waits for the others to nod in agreement, which they do vehemently, like Bobbleheads in an Orange County tremor. "That said, we presume you'll want to introduce her around at the next Hilldale Women's Club luncheon. You know, membership has its privileges."

"Really? No, I didn't know. Maybe someday you'll invite me to join."

The women look from one to the other. I guess it somehow slipped their minds that I'd never been invited.

Yes, I'm having fun watching them eat a little crow with their cake and coffee.

Penelope clears her throat. "I'm sure it's an oversight on someone's part. It will be rectified immediately, of course. Hayley, please make a note of it."

Hayley reaches in her purse for a pen and a tidy pad, in which she scribbles something down. I'm guessing it's REDRUM REDRUM REDRUM...

I turn to Penelope. "You said something about privileges? By any chance would those include a vacation from school carpool for, say, the next month?"

Penelope's eyes narrow. She mutters something under her breath (I'm guessing an expletive), but comes to her senses before saying it out loud. Carpool duty is a small price to pay, should I reel in Babette for her.

"I'm sure Tiffy and Hayley can arrange something."

Her lackeys wince, but they know the drill.

Now that the ball is in my court, they head for the door. "The luncheon is Monday, one o'clock, the grand salon at Chez Chien Lunatique."

For their benefit, Jack wraps his arms around me as I wave good-bye.

For my benefit, he doesn't laugh at the fact I'm now roped into some silly club, which only wants me as a member because I'm their connection to the most renowned trophy wife in town.

I'm sure Babette would trade that notoriety for a few real friends, and a husband who adored her instead of mocked her.

She may not find this in the Hilldale Women's Club, but if it gets her out from under Breck's thumb for a couple of hours, I'm sure she'll be just as willing to fake a friendship or two.

CHAPTER 7

DEALING WITH AWKWARD MOMENTS

Despite a hostess's attempt to assure her guests mingle well and have a marvelous time, someone is bound to do, or say, something, which makes everyone else feel a bit uncomfortable. Should that occur at your party, the best way to make amends is to laugh off the offense.

Payback comes later. In a dark alley. With a lead pipe.

At the next party, the loudmouth will behave as if the cat got his tongue (which may be the case, after you're done with him).

Supposedly, the best divorce lawyer in all of Orange County is Alan Shore, of the law firm Young, Frutt & Berluti. "Best" is another way of saying every ex-wife in the county swears by him, and every ex-husband in the county swears at him, or whenever Alan's name is uttered out loud.

This makes him the perfect attorney to represent me in my divorce.

I hand him a copy of the most recent picture I have of Carl. Considering his ability to disguise himself, I'm sure this is an exercise in futility. Besides, the picture is tiny, taken from an antique locket I wear around my neck.

Don't ask me why I keep the picture in there. I guess it reminds me of better, simpler times. When I was married to a man I loved and trusted.

Those days are long gone.

Obviously, I can't divulge everything about our break-up. For example, since Carl was never legally declared dead, I can't use that as the basis for a divorce. What I can do, is say that he deserted me five years ago.

"Gone? For five years? Great," Alan crows. "Abandonment makes it a slam dunk for you to keep the rug rats! Do you know where he is now?"

Hmmmm. Tricky question. The real Carl is on the FBI's and Interpol's most wanted list, so my guess is finding him is a long shot. The fake Carl, my Jack, is part of the Breck foursome at the Hilldale Country Club with Hans, Franz and Breck. Needless to say, I don't want a process server anywhere near him, since I haven't yet broken the news to him of my divorce filing. I'm waiting to surprise Jack with the news that I'm a free woman, when no one—specifically Carl—can stand between us.

I bat my eyes, feigning hurt and innocence. "Let's just say he's long gone. I presume we can file in abstention?"

Alan stops mid-happy dance. "What's the fun in that? This can be a real booyah!"

Um... no.

"Look, Alan, here's the thing. I want to fast-track this divorce. I don't care if it's not a fun thing for you. This isn't some high-profile, he said-she said. There will be no 'booyah' moments. I just want you to file the paperwork and follow through."

Alan's pomp deflates somewhat. "Yeah, okay, I hear you. But, lady, if you seriously want this to move at anything other than a snail's pace, we have to at least make an attempt to find him."

"Sure, okay, tell you what, if by some miracle he shows up in the next seventy-two hours, he's all yours."

"Booyah!" he shouts.

How did I know he was going to do that?

At four hundred bucks an hour, I don't have time for this nonsense.

Besides, I've got a ladies' lunch to attend with my new bestie.

"I don't know why I said I'd join you. Truthfully, I should be finalizing the menus for the summit with our chef." Babette sounds guilty as she slides into the passenger seat of my car. "But Jonah insists I go. He thinks I should take advantage of this opportunity to meet some of 'the natives,' as he calls you and the others down the hill. Besides, Edwina has everything under control. She always does."

"I'm sure the pressure has been incredible on all of you. You won't regret it. The 'natives' are friendly, I promise." Famous last words.

I look behind me as I steer down the long driveway leading out of Lion's Lair. Seems we have an escort. Although I could do it easily once we hit the mean streets of Hilldale, I fight the urge to lose Babette's security detail. "Besides, those kinds of business details are Edwina's job, aren't they?"

"Yes, of course." She sighs. "But Edwina takes on so much and never complains. I'd hate it if she ever left Jonah."

"Wow, I guess if she's that efficient, he really is lucky to have her."

"No, I'm lucky to have her, too. His last three assistants were whores."

Her harsh words cause me to run a red light. Babette's security detail sails through it, too. Unfortunately, Breck's men in the black SUV get pulled over by Officer Fife. I can't help but smile at the thought of how they'll try to bully him, and only make matters worse for themselves. He's itching to use that one bullet he's been issued for his pop gun.

"I take it, then, you didn't like them much."

"That's an understatement! It's hard to think well of someone when you find them in bed with your husband." Babette's voice shakes with anger. "It's why I find it so difficult to make friends. If they don't want something from me, they give freely of themselves—to him."

What can I say to that? Absolutely nothing.

Babette shrugs off my silence. "Don't worry, Donna. I know you're different. Edwina showed me the security feed of my husband's attack on you." I glance over just in time to see her eyes tear up. "Since I'm sitting here now, I presume you're not pressing charges, which would be the death of the summit—and my marriage."

"I know how important the summit is, Babette. I wouldn't do anything to stop it." Just the opposite, in fact. Not that I can say that to her.

As if reading my mind, she pats my arm.

So, Edwina saw the security feed prior to Arnie erasing me on it, and she showed it to Babette, as opposed to covering for her boss? Interesting, to say the least. I can't wait to hear what Jack and Ryan think of this.

I hit the gas. Now that I'm free to go the speed limit, we may actually make the meeting on time. The sooner we get there, the sooner we can leave.

Something tells me Babette will be of like mind after a half-hour with the sure-to-be fawning Penelope and her Hilldale coven.

A half hour? It only takes ten minutes for Babette's worse fears to be realized.

"We've all been dying to meet you," Penelope gushes, practically pushing me out of the way as she takes Babette in hand. Immediately, she introduces her all around. The way the members of the women's club are ooohing and ahhhhing at her reminds me of the Munchkins when Glinda the Good Witch arrives in her bubble.

Or in Babette's case, a Toyota Highlander Hybrid.

Oh, what a world, what a world.

Seeing that Penelope has already seated Babette in the chair next to hers and that the rest of the chairs around their table are already taken, I tap Hayley on the shoulder to point this out. "Where am I supposed to sit?"

Hayley smirks as she points to an easel, which holds a bulletin board. "The seating chart is over there."

"Thanks." For nothing.

I walk over the board. I have to scan it twice before finding my name. I'm placed at a half-filled table, in the Siberia between the ladies' room and the kitchen door. Figures.

If this were high school, it would be branded the loser's table—not that I'd say that to my tablemates. The way they're sucking down their mojitos, I'm guessing they've already figured this out.

"My name is Carla Fontaine," says a woman with a squalling baby. "And this is Lucinda Manley." She points to a woman who tops out at over three hundred pounds, a crime in a room filled the anorexically challenged. "And Tara Wills."

From the looks of things, Tara's social faux pas is that she's got the figure and the face of a human Barbie doll. Oh yeah, and her top is open to her navel. Tara tilts her head at me. "Carla's sitter bailed on her, Lucinda is fine with her weight, and

Penelope's idiot husband once made a pass at me. So, what put you on Penelope's shit list?"

I flop down beside Lucinda. "So many reasons, so little time."

In order to kill the next couple of hours, I am tempted to stick my head in the pitcher of mojitos, but I'm stopped by the buzz of my cell phone. It's a text message from Emma:

Time 2 take out trash! UK hardy OK poolside at HD 4Seas!

In other words, there has been a confirmed sighting of one of Asimov's possible assassins. The Ukrainian hard man known as Oleksaner Kovalenko has officially been spotted in Hilldale, and he's hanging at the Four Seasons. Should he die of natural (or for that matter, any) causes, no one would blink an eye.

That's where I come in. I'm his designated angel of death.

"So sorry, family emergency," I say to my tablemates. They toast my luck in having the only excuse to leave in which Penelope must forgive.

I give the same excuse to Babette, murmuring in her ear, "It's Jeff. He forgot to take his basketball uniform to school. I'll be back before this is over. I promise."

"And if she's not, we'll be happy to give you a lift home," Hayley offers breathlessly.

Babette winces. I'm leaving her with a den of wolves, and she knows it.

That's okay. If I don't accomplish my mission, she'll have a bigger reason to be disappointed in me.

Arnie has no trouble breaking into the Four Seasons' reservation software. The security feed, which shows Oleksaner going to his room on the second floor near the back exit, allows Acme to determine his room number and the alias with which he signed in.

James Bond.

In his dreams.

The employee locker room in the Four Seasons is easy to find. What I'm looking for are the uniforms worn by the cocktail waitresses who serve the patrons sitting poolside. I find one. It's short, sweet, and nautically themed. I put the hat at a jaunty angle on top of my short, blond wig, leave on my very tall heels, and head toward the sun and fun.

It's a good thing he's decided to catch a few rays. Otherwise, his pasty complexion would stand out during the summit, since most of the power players attending will be sporting golfing tans.

Oleksaner is easy to spot. Like most men from anywhere else but the United States (excluding the US Olympic Swim and Rowing teams) he's in a Speedo. It's so tight that I am reminded of a two-pound salami in a one-pound bag. Okay, make that a half-pound of salami in a quarter-pound bag. They say most hit men have something to prove. I think I can guess Oleksaner's hang-up.

Since he's just gotten out of the pool, he can always claim shrinkage, but his waitress isn't buying it. She shrugs when he tosses out a come-on line with his drink order.

I watch as the bartender mixes his drink: a whisky sour. Perfect. He'll never taste the concentrated aconite I'll add to it from my pinky ring. This plant-based poison hits its victims like a heart attack.

When the bartender turns to take care of three more orders, I make my move. The setting on my ring is flipped palm-side, allowing me to snap it open with my thumb and release the poison even as I saunter over to Oleksaner, who is scoping out the poolside cuties.

But just as I'm about to set his drink on the table beside his chaise, he lowers mirrored Ray-Bans to give me the once-over. "What happened to other girl?" His Slavic snarl doesn't mask his suspicion.

"She got a headache, and I'm looking for tips." To make my point, I bend down provocatively and squeeze my cleavage so that it practically bulges out of my uniform's tight sailor top.

He slips a fiver between my breasts.

Wait a minute! I let him cop a feel, and I don't even get enough tip money to get my car out of the Four Season's parking lot? What a cheapskate.

I don't give him a backward glance when I hear him gurgling his last breath.

By the time the hotel staff figures out he's not sleeping, he should be nice and tan.

Lucky me, I make it back to the Hilldale Women's Club just as the luncheon is breaking up. Penelope glowers at me. I guess she was hoping I wouldn't make it back in time, and she'd have the chance to see Lion's Lair up close. Well, too bad. All I need is for her to barge in, what with all the chaos that may ensue.

For some reason, the whole room is giving Babette a standing ovation. Seeing me, Babette walks over and gives me a hug.

"You were right! They really aren't so bad," she seems relieved.

"What just happened," I shout to her over the clapping.

"Oh, nothing, really. I just invited everyone to President Asimov's welcoming reception. Jonah likes a packed house, especially when it's filled with fawning female acolytes."

"Wow, that's... great." Yep, it's just what Breck needs.

And just what I need, a roomful of witnesses who can identify me, if and when I have to take out a baddie.

Unless I can talk her into making the event a masked ball. Now, there's a thought.

Pleased the luncheon was more air kisses than unsheathed claws, Babette says, "You and Trisha are welcomed to accompany your husband through the duration of the summit. Jonah is so appreciative you've taken me under your wing. Please say yes."

She's more right than she knows.

Still, the way she says this gives me the creeps. I'm not some prize.

Not for Jonah Breck, anyway.

Certainly Babette's invitation, coupled with Oleksaner Kovalenko's sudden demise, will put me back in Ryan's good graces. But the intel Emma is collecting still has him worried. The Russian dissident and Chechen assassin are still out there somewhere, and it's odd to have all three after the same target.

Something's just not right.

CHAPTER 8

HOW TO KEEP A SLEEPOVER FROM

BEING A YAWN

Popularity has its price: you are wanted and fêted at all hours of the day and night! When invited to a sleepover, be sure to pack all the essentials: jammies and slippers, toothbrush and toothpaste, face cream and night mask, shampoo and hot iron.

And most importantly, a plastic mattress cover and stun gun. By covering the mattress, you'll stop any unwanted critters from hopping onto you. However, should the critter be human, stun first, ask questions later, and conveniently remove in the plastic bag. Remember to zip it good and tight!

"If it's okay with Aunt Phyllis, can Cheever and Morton stay over on the first night you and Dad and Trisha are at that big shindig up the hill?" Jeff's question is delivered with his secret weapon: puppy dog eyes.

He looks just like Carl does—I mean did—after we had sex.

How can I say no to him?

The least I can do is try. The last thing Aunt Phyllis needs while babysitting Mary and Jeff is two more ten-year-old boys raising all sorts of hell around the house.

I shake my head. "No. Absolutely not."

"But, Mom, why not?" Jeff whines. "Trisha will be gone, too, so it shouldn't be any trouble for Aunt Phyllis."

"I'm sure Aunt Phyllis will welcome more bonding time with you and Mary."

Aunt Phyllis shrugs. "Nah, I'll be bored out of my gourd. All Mary does is yap on her cell phone. Besides, how many times can I whup Jeff at Diablo III?"

Jeff winces when he hears that. "Oh yeah? Well, I bet you can't beat Morton."

A devious smile lights up Aunt Phyllis's face. "You're on. In fact, I'll bet a five note, from each of you."

I'm outnumbered again. No surprise there.

This turn in the conversation is enough to tear Mary away from her ceaseless texting. "If Jeff is having a sleepover, can I have one, too?"

I shake my head adamantly "No! Absolutely, positively not!"

"Jeff gets to have his dweeby friends over, and I can't? Dad, please tell Mom she's not being fair!"

Jack looks up from his computer. He's been trying to bone up on the latest catchphrases being tossed around by the international financial community. Last night he tried a few of them on me. I got him to stop when I pointed out that terms like "financial repression" and "quantitative easing" weren't exactly the kind of naughty talk that put me in the mood. To minimize any risk to hot hanky-panky, he quickly shut his yap, and instead we engaged in some high-frequency trading of kisses and foreplay maneuvers. In no time at all, the velocity of interconnection between us led to a thorough and fully satisfying systematic inclusion, which left us both panting.

"Now, that was one insider trading violation," I gasped.

I guess I'm picking up some of the lingo after all. Pays to stay after school with teacher.

Until teacher sells you out.

"What... a sleepover? I don't mind, Mary, honey—if it's okay with Aunt Phyllis, of course."

Aunt Phyllis gives Jack a thumbs-up. "Sure, the more, the merrier!"

I give up. Time to pack my overnight bag.

As I walk past him, Jack murmurs in my ear, "Hey, I don't know about you, but I could use a little hyperinflation."

I wave him off as I head toward the stairs. "After that selloff? Dream on."

By the time we get to Lion's Lair, already twenty of the twenty-two heads of state have arrived, as well as CEOs of the five largest international media conglomerates, and representatives from eight of the world's largest financial institutions.

POTUS won't be arriving for another three days, whereas Asimov's helicopter will be here any moment now. Everyone is getting ready for the black-tie dinner to welcome him.

Hopefully, the other two assassins won't also be in attendance.

The sooner we find out where they are, the better. Arnie has been able to download the summit's guest room manifest. Audio bugs are in the floral bouquets that have been placed in the rooms of guests who are staffers of the heads of state. Despite the guards' face-to-eye scan vetting of all guests, vendors and staff, Acme's facial photographic analysis software has yet to make a match to the visages of the two hard men still on the loose.

The Breck's au pair, Antoinette, immediately takes Trisha in hand. As far as Trisha is concerned, she's in My Little Pony heaven. For the next few days, we'll be just an afterthought.

How convenient. Our bedroom suite is on the same floor and wing as Breck's master bedroom and office.

As I get out of the shower, I notice that Jack is already dressed in his tux. "Considering Asimov lands in less than an hour, if an assassin is here, we don't have much time to take him out," Jack says. "I guess I should head downstairs to introduce myself to some guests, and to do some recon."

He hesitates just long enough to gaze down at my naked, damp body. I know he's thinking how easy it would be to pull me down onto that king-sized bed. How fun it would be for me to undress him. How he aches to be inside me.

Well, if he's not thinking this, he should be.

I get my answer when he draws me in close. As he leans in to give me a kiss, his lips linger over mine.

"Soon," I whisper, and the spell is broken.

He sighs, then heads out, closing the door behind him.

I've just started to dry my hair when I hear a knock. I grab my robe and tie it around me before answering the door. I presume it's a servant with our extra towels.

Abu is standing there. He still has Eddie in his arms. "Ah, Mrs. Stone! Your daughter asked I retrieve her bear from you," he says in a conversational tone.

"Why, thank you," I respond. "Please come in." But before I usher him in, I turn on my iPod to an Elvis Costello song, then shut the bathroom door. This signals Arnie to loop an innocuous twenty seconds of pre-recorded empty room digital footage, so that the covert surveillance camera won't pick up what's happening.

I run to the door to let Abu in. When Eddie starts to whine, Abu picks up the dog and muzzles him. "This job is driving me crazy! This mutt has a mind of his own." As he sits down on the bed, the dog licks his beard. "Why do I get the feeling he's just looking for crumbs?" He shakes his head in disgust. "Hey, listen.

Emma just texted with a tip on the Chechen. Apparently, our target is one of the good guys, part of a rebel group, which calls itself the Gray Wolf Brigade. Its operatives have a tiny tattoo of a wolf on the inside of their wrists."

I pet Eddie, who immediately rolls over to get his belly scratched. "It's not much of a lead. I guess if we shake enough hands, we may uncover our target."

"For now, it's all we've got." Abu scratches his beard. "I think this darn dog has fleas."

"It's your imagination. Eddie's got to be the best kept dog in the world. Which reminds me: I saw a Nova episode on the intelligence of dogs. Seems that they take their behavioral cues from us. If we're happy, so are they."

Abu shakes his head helplessly. "Then this dog must want to jump off a cliff."

"The point I'm trying to make, Abu, is that you should watch how Eddie responds to those around him. For example, does he act differently when Janie is happy or sad, or if Babette seems harried?"

"Nothing like when Breck is in the room! Then Eddie goes bonkers. The growling is unbelievable."

Yeah, well, he's not the only one who tenses up around the lord and master of the manor. Not that I'd say that to Abu. "Have Arnie's toys been of any help?"

"Nope. This pooch is stubborn. Refuses to shut up, no matter how many times I push Arnie's squeeze toy silencer. I've tried bribing and scolding. Babette has already warned me that they aren't pleased with my results. They're afraid Eddie is going to bite some head of state. I just hope I can hold onto my gig until this shindig is over."

"Do yourself a favor and download that Nova program. Maybe it'll give you a clue as to what you're supposed to be doing."

"Aye, aye, boss lady." As he salutes me with one hand, he opens the door with the other. Big mistake. Eddie, seeing his chance at freedom, races down the hall.

"Dog whisperer my ass," Abu mutters, as he takes off after his charge.

I've just clicked on the dryer again, when there's another knock on the door. I crack it open to find a maid standing there, with an armful of towels. "Shall I take them into the bathroom, Madame?" Her accent is slightly British, which is par for the course around here.

"No, that's okay. I'll take them."

She smiles and hands them to me.

That's when I see it—a small tattoo of a wolf on her left arm.

Her eyes follow mine. She senses I know who she is.

Her arm comes up toward my face. I block it with my forearm, then kick her in the gut. She falls back, slamming into the dresser. This stuns her, but just for a second. She reaches behind her and yanks the dryer from the electrical socket. In no time at all, she's got the cord wrapped around both her wrists and arms.

"You won't stop me from killing him." Her vow is soft, but deadly. "With what he's done to others like me? That pig does not deserve to live!"

"Trust me I get it. But it's not happening here, or now."

We both know I can't talk her out of her mission anymore than she can talk me out of mine: to save Asimov's sorry ass.

We circle each other warily, assessing each other's weaknesses: She's got more bulk than me, but she's also slower. I'm taller, too. Best yet, I'm now up against the dresser. Obviously, she considers this a weakness because she charges me.

Even with the cord wrapped around my neck, all it takes is one squirt of my spray cologne in her eyes to blind her.

She stumbles into the bathroom, dragging me with her into the shower, where she turns on the water, full force. She's hoping to wash the sting out of her eyes.

What she doesn't count on is my ability to kick her into the shower.

She bangs her head against the marble wall. Before she comes to her senses, I untangle myself from the cord, plug the dryer into an electrical socket, and throw it into the tub.

Wolverine's death mask stare and the smell of her frying skin sends me gagging from the room followed by a shower of sparks as the electrical system shorts out.

I shut the bathroom door, then lay down on the bed to catch my breath.

This time when there's a tap on the door, I throw it open, to let Jack in.

But no. It's Jonah Breck.

I pull my robe tightly around me. "My husband is out right now."

He smirks. "I know, dear. That's why I'm here. Don't worry, we've got all the time in the world. He's with the Japanese defense minister, who is somewhat long-winded." From behind him, he pulls a bottle of Tattinger's and two champagne glasses. "I presume you're finding your accommodations to your liking."

"In all honesty, there's a short in the bathroom's electrical system—"

Before I can say another word, he has backed me onto the bed. When my robe falls open, he whips the sash out from around me. Before I know it, he's flipped me onto my stomach.

"I could use that drink right now," I gasp, as he binds my wrists with the sash.

"We'll celebrate afterward." I hear him fumbling with his zipper. "You will, anyway. Trust me, I'll have you begging for more."

Promises, promises.

I struggle and try to sweet talk some sense into him, but no use. He's got me pinned. I've just about given up any hope of the Calvary coming when there is a sharp knock on the door.

"Mrs. Stone?" Both Breck and I recognize Edwina's voice. "Mrs. Stone, your daughter requests you come immediately."

"Answer her." Breck's hot breath sears my ear.

I shout, "I'll—I'll be right there."

"I'll have to escort you. The girls are eating in the south wing media room tonight, and with security as tight as it is... Well, you can just imagine."

Breck mutters a curse as he rolls off me. Even as he unties me with one hand, the other gently follows the curve of my ass—

When he smacks it hard, I swallow the urge to cry out.

"A love tap. There's more where that came from. You'll love the tour of my dungeon."

He's got a dungeon? His corporate bio doesn't mention a sadistic streak, but yeah, okay, makes sense.

I leap up and grab my dress, which is hanging over the chair.

Breck smiles as I struggle into it. "Allow me to zip you up."

I suppress a shudder at the thought of his hands anywhere on me. Instead, I nod.

He presses the zipper into my skin as he inches it up, ever so slowly. When he's done, I feel his lips grazing my neck. They linger there as he breathes in the scent of my skin, sweat, and disgust.

How I long to smash that champagne bottle over my host's head, but seriously, what kind of guest would that make me?

And besides, I can't deal with the disposal of two dead bodies tonight.

Before I leave, I flip off Elvis Costello.

I can just imagine Ryan and Arnie's shock and awe at seeing Breck slithering out of the room.

I don't even want to think about Jack's reaction.

Let alone what he'll say about the fried maid in the shower. I guess I have a lot of explaining to do.

"I've got a pretty good sense of direction," I say to Edwina. "We aren't headed to the south wing, are we?"

Edwina, somewhat embarrassed, shakes her head. "I presumed you needed... some fresh air."

She ushers me out to a terrace. The sun is setting. From here, we can actually see directly into the ballroom, where many of the guests have already gathered in anticipation of President Asimov's arrival.

I turn to face her. "Thank you, Edwina. Please tell me, how did you know Breck was in my room?"

She shrugs. "He's predictable. You're available. Or at least, he's arrogant enough to think so. Even if you put up a fight, he presumes your husband will make you do whatever is necessary to make his deal. Most of them do."

I can only imagine.

"He had me put you close by," she continues. "But after he attacked you in his office, I felt it necessary that I keep an eye on him."

"Babette mentioned you'd shown her the security feed." I shake my head in wonder. "Why doesn't she divorce him?"

"She has no alternative. If she leaves, he'll see to it that she never sees Janie again." Edwina's voice trembles. "It sickens her, but his infidelities are a small price to pay."

"I see now why she'd put up with it. But you're not like his other lackeys, who find it easy to look the other way. Tell me, Edwina, what's your excuse?"

Instead of answering, she gazes out over the horizon. "Ah, look. President Asimov has arrived. By the time they're settled, the reception will have already started. I must meet him and his security team, to show them to their quarters."

She's right. The helicopters are still far enough away they can't be heard, but they can be seen, if barely.

"You still have the time to answer me."

"I owe Mr. Breck my life." Her smile is slight, and not happy at all. "Now if you'll excuse me, I have to alert him as to our guest of honor's arrival."

So, both of the women in Breck's life feel tethered to him, despite hating his guts.

As she walks off, all I can think of is how badly I want this mission to be over, so that I can divorce Carl. That way, Jack and I can get on with the rest of our lives.

CHAPTER 9

DEALING WITH A PARTY CRASHER

Big parties come with big headaches. One of the worst is the party crasher because he fraternizes with the guests, eats the food you've so carefully chosen and prepared, guzzles your liquor, and upsets your seating chart.

So, how should you eliminate him without making a scene? Easy! Slip a roofie into his drink, declare him drunk or tired from "over-exertion," and call a taxi to take him—

To the city dump.

A great hostess always keeps the trash out of sight, and out of mind.

"I see you had company while I was out," Jack murmurs in my

ear, as we dance, cheek to cheek in the grand ballroom, which takes up the whole top floor of Lion's Lair.

For an hour now, a twenty-piece orchestra has been playing classic pop tunes. Excitement is in the air, but the natives are getting restless. While some of the swells make tepid attempts to be great sports and escort the handful of ladies around the dance floor, most of the movers and shakers congregate in clusters, like penguins staking out their territorial icebergs.

The security guards are also in tuxedos, but you can tell who they are by the way they talk to themselves, or tilt their heads and tap their ears in order to listen to any internal chatter on possible threats.

Despite my gritted teeth, I give Jack—and any camera pointed our way—a dazzling smile. "You betcha, lots of company. In fact, so many people knocked on the damn door, I felt I was in that Marx Brothers movie. You remember the one: where everyone crams into a tiny stateroom?"

"Ah, yes, A Night at the Opera. Comic genius, lots of shenanigans!" Jack dips me to the floor. "But for some reason, I don't remember a dead maid in that one."

"Maybe you didn't look closely enough. Speaking of up close and personal, your cheering squad just walked in."

What I see upside down, and he now notices right side up, is the entrance of Penelope and the rest of the club's members, all with spouses in tow. The men wear the requisite tuxedos, while the women are dressed in a rainbow array of couture gowns. Christmas came early to Hilldale's Bergdorf-Goodman, Saks Fifth Avenue and Nordstrom. I can only imagine the two-day grabfest that went on as the women's club members picked over the racks.

There are no black eyes, but I haven't had a chance to peruse the Hilldale Police Department's arrest reports, either. If jail time has been served, any and all perpetrators have made it out in time for the most memorable soirée in Hilldale's history.

"Lucky me," he says, as he pulls me back into his arms. "I think they have a new crush."

Despite the fact Jonah Breck greets Penelope by brushing her proffered hand with his lips, it must be a crushing disappointment for her to discover that, for the most part, the other women invited aren't socialites or wives of the powerful, but the arm charm variety: young, stunningly beautiful, and well-displayed. In Breck's eyes, Penelope Bing's well-toned yummy mommy body trussed up in a colorful Roberto Cavalli print is no match for the tight, nude-toned plunging gown worn by Babette's personal shopper, Marilyn, with whom Breck is now doing a hip-to-hip cha-cha.

After what I've seen of Breck, I now know why Babette couldn't care less who fills his dance card.

When the orchestra starts the overture to the ballad Someone to Watch Over Me, Jack pulls me close. It would be nice to just lay my head on his broad chest, but duty calls. Jack's head is angled to scan the room, leaving me to watch the grand staircase.

And that's when I see him.

Carl, my soon-to-be ex.

Smiling down at me, he walks down the staircase and through the crowd toward us. Tall, dark and broad shouldered, his deep green eyes assess, even as they seem to ignore.

Or appreciate. No wonder the heads of every woman he

passes turns to watch and admire. It's instinctive, this desire we women have, to run toward the strongest and most virile of our species.

In my case, the urge is to run away from him. Then again, I'm the only one in the room who knows how he treats his loved ones.

I've got the bullet scar to prove it.

When he reaches us, he taps Jack on the back in order to cut in. "May I?" he has the audacity to ask.

I give Jack credit. He doesn't do a double-take. However, his eyes display disbelief by opening wider before they narrow in anger.

Nor does he punch Carl, let alone stab or shoot him.

I guess he's relieved I haven't done anything stupid, either.

Not yet, anyway.

As Carl whisks me away, he holds me tight. Too tight. "Honey, I'm home," he murmurs into my ear. "Did you miss me?"

"Not at all. In fact, I was hoping you'd crawled into some hole and died of internal bleeding."

"Don't flatter yourself. You're not that great a shot." Carl shrugs. "You have that habit of angling slightly to the right. Gotta watch that, babe. Unless...Whoa, wait a minute! You really didn't mean to take me down, now, did you?" He pulls back slightly, in order to watch my expression.

Okay yeah, it's a gotcha moment. "Screw you, Carl."

"I knew it!" He's practically crowing. "Still carrying a torch for ol' Carl. Has lover boy figured this out yet?"

I try to pull away, but he won't let me. "Don't flatter yourself. I was handicapped, remember? You had just winged me in the shoulder."

"Yeah well, I guess we were both a little off our game that day." He concedes with a sheepish nod. Then he jerks me even closer and leans into me. Sure, okay fine. I shift closer, forcing him to follow me in a figure eight tango, shifting my leg so that it hooks onto his before it climbs slowly to his upper thigh.

Carl smirks, impressed. "When did you learn to tango?"

"From Jack. He taught me well, don't you think?"

He nods, grudgingly. "Everyone needs a hobby."

"What's yours?" I can only imagine. Bangkok hookers? No, too obvious. It's got to be the joy of making my life miserable.

As if reading my mind, he answers, "Resurrection."

It's on the tip of my tongue to say that there would be no need for a resurrection, if you'd stayed with me. And if you hadn't been seduced by the Quorum's quest for power. And if you hadn't faked your death and deserted me and the kids.

Seeing the look on my face, he's all grins. "Lighten up! I heard James Bond say it, in a 007 movie. I swear, sometimes I think the producers are following me around with a camera—"

"You son of a bitch!" I shove him away. "Oh, boy, I am so outta here."

I start to walk away, but he won't let go of my hand, yanking me toward him, into a tight squeeze. In this position, his lips easily nuzzle my neck. "Admit it. We still make beautiful music together. This has got to be driving Jack crazy."

"You better pray it isn't. In any regard, you're a dead man the minute you leave this room."

"Don't bet on it. I'm quicker and smarter than he is."

"What the hell are you doing here, anyway?" I ask, crossly. "Have you forgotten you're on the Interpol and FBI watch lists?"

"Tell me the truth. Do you think my wanted poster does me justice? It makes me look so... I don't know, mean, I guess. Like a bad guy or something."

I shake my head. "The only photo I'd want to see is one taken from a morgue, with a bullet right between your eyes."

"Tsk, tsk. Bitter does not become you, Donna. But that dress... it certainly does."

His gaze, filled with desire, has me blushing. I want to push him away, but he holds me close, rocking me side to side with the rhythm of the music. "You know, he could have killed me, but he didn't."

"When? What are you talking about?"

"After Anaheim. He tracked me down, in Montenegro. Fuck it if I know how he did it. Had me in his sights, too. I felt him, but I didn't see him until it was too late. Like Bambi, in headlights..." His voice trails off. "Only, he didn't pull the trigger."

I know Jack better than that. "You're lying, Carl."

"Hey, if I hadn't been there myself, I wouldn't believe it, either. Why don't you ask him? When you do, let me know what he says. My guess is that he realized if he took me out, deep down, you'd never forgive him."

"You're wrong. What I want more than anything is you out of my life."

"Sorry to disappoint you, but that ain't going to happen. So, what do you say we kiss and make up?"

He tips my chin up and comes in close. I can't pull a gun now, in front of all these witnesses. But I could bite his tongue off. It's a drastic way to make him shut the hell up, but hey, it would certainly do the trick.

Before I have time to react, his mouth is on mine, and his tongue is deep down my throat.

My hand grabs the bulge in his Armani tux, and I hear him gasp. The sound is music to my ears. "You're the hitter, aren't you?"

He winces in pain, but he's still able to mutter, "What the hell are you talking about?"

"Alexei Asimov. You're here to take him out, aren't you?"

"What? You think I'm the—the shooter? Hell no, babe! I'm the consultant heading up Asimov's security team."

He's laughing so hard at my shock and awe that I almost lose my grip on him.

Almost, but not quite.

When I walk off the dance floor, I've left him doubled over, and not because he's still laughing at me.

CHAPTER 10

HOW TO BE THE PERFECT GUEST

It's your turn to enjoy the hospitality of others! Your drive to be the consummate hostess also provides you with insights on how to be the ideal guest.

For example, if the hostess seems overwhelmed, offer to lend a hand. Choose a task in which your expertise will make it quick and simple: say, setting a table, arranging flowers, or diffusing a bomb. Your hostess will certainly appreciate your efforts, and compliment you on your handiwork.

Remember: guests never overstay their welcome, so do not be the last one out the door—especially if you fail at dismantling the bomb, and it is due to go off before the party is over.

Alexei Asimov is one smooth-talking dude.

His voice caresses and inspires. His compliments about our "heavenly Hilldale" are eloquent, drawing ahhhhs and applause from the locals, who have no desire to reconcile today's graciousness with a fiendish curriculum vitæ filled with decades of brutality.

His vow to do his part for "eternal peace on Earth" earns him a standing ovation. I can only imagine the onslaught of frenzied hysteria that filled his ears when, in the Ukraine, he gave his machine gun-toting army the command to fire at those who had just dug their own mass graves.

Put a man in a tux, call him a statesman, and all is forgiven.

Carl stands just behind Asimov, to his right. A second member of the Russian security team is to his left. I spot others, every ten feet or so, mumbling, sotto voce, into well-hidden headsets.

Jack is also muttering, to Ryan. Cursing, really. Ryan has just informed us that Carl's role on Asimov's advance team has given him diplomatic immunity.

In other words, he's been removed from the Terrorist Screening Database, as well as all international security watch lists.

That still doesn't get him off my personal shit list.

"But what if Asimov is being set up by the Quorum, and Carl's the shooter we've been looking for all along?" Jack asks.

"Listen, you two, I don't like it, either." Ryan's bitterness is merited. He recruited and trained Carl for Acme. It was on his watch that Carl was turned by the Quorum.

Ryan sighed deeply. "Until Carl makes his move, we have to give him the same leeway as any of the others on Asimov's security detail. This mission depends on staying close enough to Asimov to protect him, especially if the hit is going to be an inside job. Donna, if that means turning on the charm so that Carl accommodates us, do it."

Jack and I exchange glances. It's not what either of us wants to hear. I know I don't have to reassure him of this, but I press his hand to my lips anyway.

Yes, I know Carl is watching us, but I don't give a damn.

"And if it turns out you're right and Carl's the inside man," Ryan adds, "you've both got your orders: shoot to kill."

The ghost of a smile accompanies Jack's slight nod.

Not that he needs Ryan's permission to do so. And if what Carl said is right—about Jack letting him walk because he thinks I'd hate him for taking Carl out—then I've got to let him know that he has my permission, too.

If I don't kill Carl first.

The father of my children is also a menace to society. I may not be able to change his role in my kid's lives, but I can keep him from ruining our world as we know it.

"Carl told me about Montenegro."

Upon hearing this, Jack curses, then sits up in the bed. He doesn't look at me, but stares straight ahead.

Lesson learned: don't bring up your ex while basking in the afterglow of sex. Talk about a mood killer.

The moonlight streaming in from the window throws strange shadows on the wall. His profile looms large and dark. By now, I know every inch of his face so well my mind colors him in. His deep-set eyes. The tiny crook in his nose. The dimple in his chin. The way his forelock hangs forward before his large, broad hand pushes it back impatiently. His mouth has a tendency to draw up on the right side when he's about to let loose with a laugh.

But he is not laughing now. He's wondering how to answer me.

I touch his back gently, assuring him there are no wrong answers.

I hear the hurt, pain and anger expelled in his soft sigh. "As long as Carl's alive, he'll always stand between us."

"You're wrong. I'd never let that happen. I swear."

"You wouldn't, but he'd make sure of it. He'd always be there. He'll never let go of you, let alone the children. He's got too much pride for that."

Of course Jack's right.

"After what he did to you—after shooting you—I had every right to take him out. You say you'd forgive me, but let's be honest with each other. If I killed the father of your children, he wins. He'd still stand between us. Between you and me, And between Mary, Jeff and Trisha and me."

"But they don't know about him!"

He shrugged. "Life has many twists and turns. Anything can

happen to either of us. When it does—"

"You mean 'if.' And even if 'it' did happen, to one of us, the other would keep them safe. The other would be there to help them through their pain, to keep our memory alive."

"Donna, that's just it. When it comes to me, their memories are too new."

"Jack, they love you! You're the only dad they've ever known. And their memories of you are all good ones. Whatever they remember about Carl has your face on it."

"Don't you think Carl knows that? Donna, why do you think he can't stay away?"

"Don't worry, Jack. I'll take care of him."

"It's what he's counting on—that one of us comes gunning for him! It'll allow him to justify what he wants to do to us."

"No, I don't mean 'take care of him' as in kill him. Although, yeah, under the right circumstance... Listen, Jack. What I'm trying to say is I'm making it legal. I'm divorcing him."

Jack turns his head to stare at me. He's no longer in profile and the shadows hide his features in pitch darkness, but I can imagine the grin on his face, the love in his eyes.

I'm not prepared for the disbelief in his voice. "You're not serious, are you?"

"Yes, of course I am." Why isn't he doing cartwheels around the room? "I thought you'd be happy about this. I've already talked to a lawyer and explained the situation."

"Wow. I would have liked to be a fly on the wall to hear that conversation."

"Get real. Do you think I told him everything? I'm not stupid. I just told him what he needed to hear."

"Tell me! I need a good laugh." He stands up and heads to the far wall, where the shadows are the deepest. Now I can't make him out at all.

"Nothing about Carl's profession. Or mine, for that matter. Just that Carl deserted us five years ago, and I'm ready to move on."

"What will you do when your lawyer finds out you've been living with your 'husband' for the past year?"

"He won't. He's a paper pusher. We're filing in absentia. Abandonment will be the legal reason. All's well that ends well."

"Yeah, right."

"Quit being so negative! Afterward, you and I can make it legal... If you want."

Silence.

What the hell?

The room is so dark I can't even see him. But I can smell fear.

I toss a pillow at him. The smack is accompanied his grunt. "What was that for?" he mutters.

"For your head. Go sleep in the bathtub."

"There's a dead body in there, remember?" Arnie can't come and dispose of her until bright and early tomorrow morning, when he's allowed back in to collect all the dead blooms he'll be gathering throughout the estate's sixty-six rooms. In hindsight, it's the perfect way to cover up the smell of a rotting corpse.

Jack can't see my shrug. "Maybe she's your type, now that

we've established that I'm not."

"You're being silly. Of course you're my type... I mean, at least you're breathing."

"Hardee har har."

I feel him flop down on the bed beside me. But when he tries to hold me, I push him away.

"Donna, don't be angry with me. It just surprised me that you'd spoken to a lawyer before you talked to me."

"Gee, I guess I wasn't expecting you to freak out!"

"Lower your voice. I'm not freaking out. I'm... trying to process what it all means."

"It means I'll be free of him. It means we can be together." I have to blow my nose or else I'll choke on my tears, my snot and my shame. "It means we can quit pretending to be man and wife, because it'll be true."

"You realize this will make things worse between you and Carl, right?"

"He's tried to kill me. Twice. How much worse can it get?" I shrug. "Jack, tell me the real reason you're upset."

"I... I just don't know if the timing is right."

Now it's my turn to sit up in bed. "Oh? Just when will it 'be right?'"

"Wrong choice of words. Forget I said that."

I get up, taking the covers and my pillow with me to the chaise lounge by the window. "Tell you what. When you feel the time is 'right,' you let me know. Until then, we're just two operatives on an assignment. When this is over, feel free to ask for a transfer.

We'll call it a 'divorce.'"

His laugh is weak. If he's hoping I'll join in, he's got another thing coming. Finally, he stops. "You don't really mean that...do you?"

I want to say no. I want to tell him that I love him with all my heart, and that I'd die if he left me. I want to run to him and have him hold me in his arms, kiss me, and tell me that he's sorry for being a stupid idiot; that I took him by surprise, but now that it's sunk in that I'll be free to be his, and that it's his wish, too.

Instead, I say nothing.

I feel nothing.

I might as well be the corpse in the other room.

I realize now it isn't Carl who stands between Jack and me, because there never was a Jack and me.

I turn and bury my head in my pillow at the thought that, once again, the man in my life has deserted me.

Chapter 11

When the Party's Over

Some guests refuse to leave, even when no one else is left at your soirée.

If you've got a reveler who can't take your graciously subtle hints that it's time to call it quits, don't be shy about letting your feelings be known. Go ahead, pull out the heavy artillery.

Yes, I'm being serious: A tank, or a couple of missile launchers, pointed at his car, will do the trick of getting him out of your hair, your house, and your sightline—

If he runs quickly enough.

"I found him," says the voice on the other end of my cell phone.

I'm too groggy to recognize it. What time is it?

I open one eye and scan the room for a clock. The one over the fireplace says it's a few minutes after eight o'clock. Jack has already slipped out.

Good. Who needs him, anyway?

Who am I kidding?

"Hey, did you hear me?" The voice on my cell phone is getting louder, more impatient. "I said, I found your husband."

I'm too tired for games. "Which one?"

"The one you're trying to get rid of! Carl Stone."

"Oh...yeah." Now I recognize the voice. It's Alan, my lawyer. "I saw him, too. Last night."

"Jeez! Did you serve him yourself?"

"What? No."

"Too bad." Alan sounds depressed. "I left a copy of the summons, with your aunt, along with your signed papers. She didn't give them to you?"

"No, I'm... I'm staying at a friend's. He showed up over here." The thought of serving Carl has me fully awake. "Alan, I won't be able to serve him myself. You see, I'm at work. But if I give you Carl's location and schedule, you can take care of it, right?"

"Just tell me when and where, and I'll get Bulldog over there."

"Um... Bulldog?"

"My best process server. He's got a one-hundred percent success rate."

"Super! I'll text it right over."

"Booyah!" Obviously, Alan is psyched.

Okay, now I am too. "Booyah!" I shout back.

I need coffee. Or a lobotomy.

No, what I need is a divorce.

I call down to the kitchen to order breakfast in bed. I deserve it, right? It's been a hell of a week, and it's just started.

"Madame has a preference for her eggs?" the disembodied voice at the other end of the phone asks.

"Three of them: sunny side up, please. And French toast. And lots of bacon, crisp."

"Madame has a healthy appetite."

"Madame thinks you should mind your own business." I slam down the phone receiver. It's my pity party, and I'll eat if I want to.

I open the bathroom door to discover I am indeed alone. Arnie has successfully removed the corpse of the assassin maid from the bathtub. He must have done it while I slept. I wonder if Jack let him in, or if he'd already taken off before Arnie got here.

I wonder where Jack is now.

This thought has me aching for him.

I should take a cold shower, but instead I run the water just this side of hot.

I'm about to jump in when I hear a ping on my cell phone.

Emma has just texted me President Asimov's itinerary, which she pulled off the shadow feed. In the two days prior to POTUS's arrival, he will see and be seen all over Hilldale. And since Carl will have to tag along, Bulldog has several opportunities to slap him with the summons.

Today's photo ops include a ten o'clock meeting with the mayor, in which he will be given the key to the city. Then, at eleven o'clock, he'll stop by the local middle school, where he'll answer questions from Mary's class, the eighth-graders, who have been studying world geography and international current events.

After a lunch back at the Breck homestead, Asimov will meet with the press.

Babette and I will join whatever summit attendees have arrived for a sumptuous dinner. Afterward, Breck and Asimov are having a private confab with a few of them, in his office. Jack isn't invited, but by then we'll have the bug in place, thank goodness.

The following afternoon, Asimov is treating the summit's guests to a grand performance of the Kiev Ballet, which is in town for the week. Babette has arranged for the students in Janie's ballet class to attend, as well as her new BFFs, the members of the Hilldale Women's Club. Needless to say, Trisha and her friends are beside themselves. I imagine the same can be said about their mothers.

And finally, that evening, unbeknownst to Babette, Breck has arranged for a surprise birthday extravaganza for her. The theme is a circus, which will be set up somewhere on their estate.

Speaking of clowns, I text Emma a request to yank a straight-on picture of Carl off the security feed. A second later, I've received it. I pass it forward to Alan via text message, along with

Carl's whereabouts over the next couple of days.

One way or another, I'll be a free woman.

Maybe freer than I want to be.

I'm just about to jump into the shower when there is a knock on the door. This time I'm smart enough to ask, "Who is it?" before opening it.

"Your breakfast, Madame."

Yea! That was quick. I open the door—

Carl is holding my tray. "Rise and shine, sleepy head."

"Sorry, not what I ordered." I try to slam the door shut, but he's already got his foot in there. I could stomp on it, but what's the use? I've got to play nice. Ryan's orders.

With his golf shirt over khaki slacks, he'll certainly fit right in on Hilldale's well-manicured and never-mean streets. The only giveaways that he's not just another well-heeled suburban dad are those six-pack abs and his jacked biceps: a sight rarely seen in a town where desk-job paunch is more the norm.

I wrap my thin silk robe around me all the tighter with one hand, and point to the coffee table by the chaise with the other. "I didn't know you were doubling as a butler. Just drop it there. I'm sort of in a hurry. Jack and I are about to take a shower—"

Carl frowns. But yes, he hears the water running. His face goes blank for just a moment. With a smirk, he sets down the tray and kicks off his shoes before sprawling out on the bed. "Great. Get him out here. I've got something important to say, and he needs to hear it, too."

The nerve of him! I don't know what irks me more: that he's

not wearing socks and has his stinky feet on my bed, or that he's about to catch me in a lie. "Jack is—he's indisposed. Just speak your mind, Carl, and then get out of here."

He pats the bed. "What's the rush? Sit down. Make yourself at home."

"Didn't you hear me? I said Jack and I are—"

"Yeah. Something about jumping into the tub together. Sounds like fun. In fact, maybe I'll join you."

He springs up and heads for the bathroom.

I run toward the door, but I'm too late. He opens it and looks around. The glass shower door reveals I'm lying to him.

Carl snickers. "What did you do, flush him down the toilet?"

"I... He...."

"Skip it. I saw him, downstairs, a half hour ago. Three's a crowd, anyway."

To prove he means this, he wraps his arms around my waist and pulls me close. I try to push him away, but his grip is like a vice, pinning me up against him. I've seen that look in his eyes before. His longing for me lights their deep, dark recesses of regret.

In the six years we were together, he learned to read me, too.

I'm sad for him, for what he's lost, and the loss still to come.

But I'm angrier that he threw it away.

Our family.

Us.

Me.

He doesn't back off from the heat of my anger. Instead, it fuels his desire all the more. I know this because his lips tell me so.

As do his hands, which gently shove my robe off my shoulders, the better to stroke my nipples. Every piece of me holds some memory of him. This is the only way I can explain why they harden under his deft touch, and why my mouth thirsts for his.

He's out of his shirt in no time. I freeze when he unbuckles his pants and they fall to the floor. When I see his thick, stiffened cock, I'm so mesmerized by the surge of emotions within me that I back away, into the shower. As the water pulses onto us, I'm blinded in a haze of steam and desire. Under the heat of his kisses, common sense melts away. I'd be lying if I said there wasn't some part of me that doesn't ache to feel him inside me again.

He was my first true love...

But now I love Jack.

And Jack loves me. Whatever reticence he feels about my upcoming divorce can't take that away.

I'm now backed up against cold marble. With all my might, I try to push Carl away. But Carl doesn't take the hint. Instead, he grinds into me. When I lift my knee as a cockblock, he takes hold of my leg and uses it as leverage to position himself so he can enter me. The look in his eye is one of lust. There is no love there, just retaliation.

This is how he takes his revenge for what he sees as my desertion.

I close my eyes in disgust—at him; more so, at myself—and brace myself for the inevitable—

Then I hear it, loud and clear: the sound of a punch is followed by a groan, smashing glass, and a body slamming into a wall.

Carl's body.

By the time I open my eyes and jump out of the shower, Jack has Carl on his back and is about to pummel his head into the bathroom's marble floor.

"Jack—Jack, don't! We didn't.... You can't!"

He freezes as if my voice has brought him to his senses, and leans back on his haunches. His chest rises and falls with pent-up adrenaline.

Make that hate.

Pained and still wary of his attacker, Carl sits up with a grunt. "Damn it, you asshole! I think you gave me a black eye."

"You're lucky I didn't kill you," Jack mutters.

"Oh, I'm not too worried about that. Not with my little insurance policy over there." Carl nods toward me. "Go ahead, Donna, hon. Tell your stooge here he had no right to break up our little party."

Jack shifts his icy stare my way. What does he read in my eyes? My guilt over a momentary lapse in judgment? My hurt over our argument last night? Would he believe I'm just following Ryan's orders to get as close as possible to the target, and his possible killer?

I wouldn't believe it, so why should he? Still, I hope so.

For just a brief second, Jack's eyes flicker with hurt before his face hardens into a mask of resignation. "Ah! I see. Sorry to have interrupted."

"That's okay. The party was over before it began." I'm not being flip, just truthful.

"Hey, wait! If you're casting aspersions on my—"

"Can it, Carl. I'm not in the mood." I'm cold, I'm hungry, and I'm naked. I reach for a towel, which remedies two of the things driving me crazy.

I can feel Jack's and Carl's eyes on me as I tighten it around me. Too bad. Show's over, boys. "You said you had something to say to us together, Carl." Despite my state of dishabille, I keep my tone business-like. "Don't leave us in suspense."

Carl attempts to rub the pain out of his jaw. "Oh yeah, before we were so rudely interrupted. Here's the dealio. The Quorum is offering a truce, through the duration of the summit."

"A truce?" I can't believe my ears. "This isn't a game of Capture the Fort. What do you take us for, fools?"

"Not at all. In fact, we find it commendable you've already exterminated two of the hitters who answered the bounty call on Asimov's head."

Jack glares at Carl. "If the Quorum didn't put the bounty on Asimov, then who did?"

"Hell if we know. But whomever it is has thought it through carefully. They've reached out to the entities who have the most to benefit from it and then gotten at least one of the hitters into Lion's Lair."

This sends a chill up my spine. "So, you think it's an inside job, too?"

"It's got to be," Carl says. "Which brings me to Acme. Asimov is also impressed with your hits—"

"Whoa, whoa, hold up here." Jack looks from Carl, to me. "Did you tell him about the interceptions?"

I shake my head.

"So, how did you know it was us?"

"Well, granted the first one threw us off, but since the second one was last seen entering this room..." He looks under the bed. Disappointed that there's nothing, or I should say no one, under there, he shrugs. "Hey, how did you get her out of the room, anyway?"

I smile innocently. "Just because you're shoveling some high-test crap doesn't mean we're going to give away our trade secrets. How we know it wasn't the Quorum who put out the hit on Asimov, in order to justify the need to hire you in the first place?"

"The protection racket? Donna, get real. We're not the Cosa Nostra. Besides, we need Asimov. When he isn't buying the Quorum's services, he's selling us the WMDs that make the world go 'round—or, inevitably, go 'boom.' If Asimov gets taken out by any other goody two-shoes who's left on his trail, we lose one big-ass kahuna."

Jack flops down into a chair. "If that's the case, why is he at the summit in the first place? He could have skipped it; stayed home to torture some more student protesters or something."

"These patty-cake sessions are par for the course. You know, make the rest of the world think the boogey man is staying in his own backyard. But in the long haul, promises are made to be broken, right? And besides, if he's here in LaLa Land, it takes the rabble's mind off the protesters."

I glance over at Jack. His nod is barely perceptible.

He may be convinced, but I'm not. "Okay, let's say we agree to this 'truce.' It doesn't mean we're going to lie down and roll over so that you can pull a fast one."

Carl's sardonic laugh sends a chill down my spine. "I'm through with the fast ones, babe. My diplomatic immunity gives me a new lease on life. In fact, after this assignment, I'm calling it quits. You know, settling down. Here in Hilldale, in fact." He smiles. "You were right, Donna. Without you and the kids, my life has been an empty shell. I'm ready to man up, be there for you."

This is a nightmare. One of us needs a wake-up call. "A shot... with me? Carl, you already took two 'shots' at me. One ended up in my shoulder! Or have you forgotten that?"

"Hey, you shot back."

Okay, yeah. He has a point.

"Marriage is tough, babe," Carl continues. "But with a little counseling, I'm guessing we'll be okay. Besides, from what I saw there in the shower, you're just as eager as I am to kiss and make up."

Jack looks like he's about to explode. His stare leaves me tongue-tied. But what am I supposed to do, blow this chance to save the target?

He walks out of the room without saying a word.

Before I find my voice, Carl leans down and kisses me on the forehead.

My love tap back to him is a punch to his gut. "Like I said,

Carl, I'm not falling for your bullshit anymore."

"Gotcha," he rasps. "I've got to earn it. Starting today."

That's what he thinks. He'll know better when Bulldog gets a hold of him.

I shove him toward the door and toss him out.

Then I go through my suitcase. What do you wear to an event where you may have to save one of the most corrupt human rights abusers in the world? I settle on a St. John tweed knit jacket and pencil skirt, worn over a scoop neck shell.

Here's hoping I don't get any bullet holes in it.

CHAPTER 12

HOW TO TREAT YOUR GUEST OF HONOR

To a hostess, every party guest is special! But above all, the person being fêted should be treated like royalty!

Besides introducing him to all the guests, he should be seated in a place of honor, usually the largest chair, or the one most centrally located in the room. At a formal sit-down dinner, it should be the one to the right of his hostess.

That way, should he get out of line or prove to be a total bore, she can easily pull the lever that drops him into her alligator moat.

The Hilldale High School marching band's rendition of Gosudarstvenny Gimn Rossiyskoy Federatsii, the Russian national anthem, hits a few sour notes. Despite this, their honored guest claps enthusiastically.

Mayor Quimby beams as the national press cameras roll, click and flash as he shakes President Asimov's hand while handing him the key to the city.

Alongside Asimov is Jonah Breck. Scanning the crowd, he sees me and licks his lips.

I try not to shiver, but I can't help it. I'm not some steak he can order. Here's hoping we spot the last assassin sooner than later, so that this mission can be over and done with.

Jack stands beside me, but he is aloof. All business. I haven't had time to explain to him that what he saw in the shower wasn't what he thinks it was. Once the divorce papers are served, he'll realize it was one big misunderstanding; that Carl was trying to get his goat.

Where is Carl, anyway?

Finally, I spot him: to the right of the crowd. His eyes shift left to right and left again. What he doesn't see is the short, bucktoothed string bean of a guy who sidles in beside him. The guy wears a T-shirt proclaiming him Single and Disease-Free.

I can guess why.

At first, Carl ignores the guy's gentle tap on his shoulder. I've got to hand it to the dude. He's persistent. Finally, Carl turns to him. I can't hear what the man is saying, but I can read his lips: Are you Carl Stone?

Carl, confused, nods slowly.

That's when the guy slaps him with the summons and shoots

off into the crowd.

So, that is Bulldog?

After watching his technique, who am I to knock his nickname? I'd say he's earned it.

Carl stares down at the paper. When he realizes what it is, he shakes his head in disbelief and smirks.

Then he sics his security team on Bulldog.

Alan's process server doesn't get far. By the time he's reached the outskirts of the crowd, he has an entourage. A couple of seven-foot thugs in dark suits and sunglasses grab hold of each arm, lifting him so high his feet can't touch the ground. Soon Carl is there, too, by their side. He yanks off Bulldog's baseball cap, stuffs the summons into it, and crams it back onto his head before they toss him into the back seat of one of their glossy black Hummers and screech off.

Damn it. So near, yet so far.

I'm about to flip open my cell phone and give Alan the bad news when Jack tosses me the keys to our car. "Edwina just called me. Breck wants me to ride back to Lion's Lair with him, so you'll have to cover the middle school event by yourself. Better get hopping. Asimov's already on the move."

He walks off without a good-bye, let alone a kiss.

Yes, that's it. Time to kiss and make-up.

We need to get on with our lives: the one we've built together, without Carl.

The Hilldale Middle School auditorium is abuzz with excitement. As Principal Belding welcomes President Asimov, the PTA chairs—Penelope, Tiffy and Hayley—are giddy enough to curtsey at him, and to hug Babette for pulling this off.

I spot Mary and her girlfriends, Wendy and Babs, in the front row. All the girls are wearing skirts and sweaters, which are half-buttoned over matching pink T-shirts. It's something I've not seen in Mary's wardrobe. I wonder when they shopped for it?

Carl and his security team cover all the exits and the balcony, where most of the parents have been sequestered. Because Carl is standing just a few feet away from the stage, he can't help but notice Mary, too. His hard stare softens at the sight of her. I can't imagine what it's like for him to see her again. Has he noticed she's a few inches taller, the different way she now wears her hair, and the natural grace that replaced her gawkiness?

Asimov's speech is short. Sadly, it's also patronizing. He uses movie clichés when describing the differences between our two countries, likening the USA to Spider-Man in that we always see bullies and feel the need to fight them. In his analogy, Russia is Batman and technology rules supreme.

"You're the bully," some eighth-grader yells from a back row. "You arrest students for speaking out against you!"

As if on cue, Mary, Babs and Wendy take off their sweaters and stand up. Written in black block letters on their pink T-shirts is the slogan Free the Pink Tacos! They chant this at Asimov, and rouse the crowd to do the same.

Asimov frowns out at the audience, which is now following their lead.

A rock song roars over the loudspeaker, but I don't understand the words because it's in Russian. I'm guessing it's the same tune that got the Pink Tacos put in prison.

Suddenly, the audience is pelting Asimov with pink taco shells.

Principal Belding is shouting for everyone to sit down and behave, as if that will do any good. Some of Asimov's security team clusters around him and nudges him off the stage. Others, Carl included, grab the girls and pull them out of the auditorium.

I run after them, but I have to fight through the reporters who have caught all of it on camera.

Here's hoping Mary's role in this public relations debacle doesn't get Jack and me kicked out of Lion's Lair.

"You almost incited a riot," Belding roars at Wendy, Babs and Mary. "You've made our school a laughing stock!"

The girls, sullen and silent, slump down deep in their chairs.

"He's right! Your daughter and her friends are a disgrace," Penelope hisses at me.

I shrug. "In our country, they have a right to protest, which is exactly the point."

"This calls for a one month suspension." Belding's tone is ominous. "If you aren't able to make up your classes, you'll repeat them in summer school."

I can't believe my ears. "This is ridiculous! What are you going to do, suspend the whole eighth grade?"

"A suspension is the last thing President Asimov would want."

Everyone turns when they hear Carl's firm, authoritative declaration, but no one says a word. I guess they're just as stunned as I am.

"The president may not like what they have to say, but he respects their right to speak their mind." Carl looks directly at Mary. "In fact, Mary, he hopes you'll be kind enough to represent your class on a one-to-one discussion with him on the issue of human rights. Would you care to join him for tea this afternoon? Your mother is also invited to come along as your escort. I'll pick you up at your home, at three."

Mary's eyes open wide as she looks over at me.

Please don't say yes, I pray silently. Please tell him that you can't stand the thought of being near that cretin.

But no. Mary, ferocious soul that she is, nods her head. "Yeah, okay, if he's willing to be honest with me, Mr. ..."

"Mr. Stone."

At first, she doesn't notice the coincidence in his name and ours. She and her girlfriends are too busy reveling in their good fortune on two counts: Belding's immediate retraction of the suspension, and Mary's invitation.

A moment later, when it finally sinks in, she looks sharply at her father, whose eyes have never left her.

I don't dare look at either of them, for fear of tearing up.

Instead, I grab Mary's hand and hustle her out the door.

"That man wasn't Russian." Mary isn't asking a question, but making a statement.

I nod. "You're right, he's an American."

"So, what's he doing with that—that dictator?"

"Asimov isn't a dictator—"

"Mom, duh, I know! Maybe not technically. But the whole world knows Russia's presidential election was rigged, and that he put anyone in jail who had the nerve to run against him. A few kids write a protest song about it and they end up doing hard labor! You call that a democracy? So, why would that man—Mr. Stone—work for him?"

"I guess he thinks it's prestigious. And I'm sure he is well paid."

"I'd never work for a sleazebag like that, no matter how much he was paying me. I have too much respect for myself."

I reach over and pat her head. "Sometimes we do things we later regret. Maybe he'll feel that way, too."

"Ha! I doubt it. He seemed so smug... or something. Like a player who thinks he knows it all." She stares out the window. Hilldale's streets in the early afternoon are quiet, but she's still running on a champion's adrenaline high. "And the way he looked at you—well, I'm just glad Dad wasn't there. He would have been soooo jealous!"

I shift uneasily in my seat. "You were imagining that."

"No I wasn't! I know love when I see it. That was the exact same look Dad gives you. I think it's hot."

Yes, Carl had love in his eyes: for her, not for me.

It's on the tip of my tongue to tell her what he wants when he sees me isn't love, but lust.

Then I think better of it. How would I explain it?

I guess I could say it's as different as... well, as Jack and Carl. But then I'd have to come clean about Carl.

Over my dead body.

Better yet, over his.

"You've done wonders with the place." Carl walks slowly through the living room, taking in everything: the soft sage walls, the deep-seated couch in front of the stone fireplace. The Persian scatter rugs over the knotty pine floors.

We picked out this house together. Up until he resurfaced last year, I'd kept its furnishings the same as the day he left.

It was a cathartic experience, throwing out everything that reminded me of him.

I shake off the compliment. "You know the saying. Life goes on." Then I head toward the stairs and shout up, "Mary? Mr. ...Mr. Stone is here! Let's get a move on!"

"Is Jeff around?" I see the glimmer of hope in Carl's eyes at the thought that he'll get to talk to his son without Jack standing between them.

I almost want to yell out Should you have the luck of getting to talk to Jeff, no matter what you say to him, Jack will always stand in your way, because you left Jeff. You left all of us.

Instead, I shrug nonchalantly. "Nope. Right about now, Aunt Phyllis is dropping him off at basketball practice."

Mary practically flies down the stairs, but freezes when she notices Carl's intense stare. "Oh! Hello, Mr. Stone. I thought you'd be waiting in the car." She's not exactly rude, but certainly cold.

Carl seems to deflate in front of my eyes.

My heart can't help but break for him.

Not Mary. He's a stranger who plays for the wrong team. As if he's not even there, she turns her back on him in order to face me. "Mom, what do you think of this dress?" It is one of her favorites: pale blue, with a crew neck, cap sleeves and a pleated skirt.

"You're beautiful," Carl murmurs.

"Oh... thanks." She gives him a dismissive wave. "Hey, would you mind being a gentleman and carrying that for me?" She points to her backpack, by the front door. She doesn't even turn to him when she says this. Instead, she keeps her eyes on me. "Mom, Dad will be there with us, right? I miss him."

Satisfied with my slow nod, she heads out the door.

Carl's smile has disappeared altogether by the time he steps outside.

Half of me wants to cry for him. But the other half wants to laugh and say, Welcome to parenting, dead-beat dad.

Instead, I say nothing. Here's hoping Mary's cruelty convinces him to stay away.

If she were to learn the truth, would she regret her actions, or feel it appropriate for a father who deserted her? The latter, I hope.

In any regard, that's the route I'm taking.

CHAPTER 13

TEA FOR TWO

A full silver tea service is a staple in every hostess's dining room! Because one never knows who will be stopping in at the appropriate time (that is to say, four o'clock). One should polish the tea service weekly, and always have the following on hand: lumps of sugar, real cream, thinly sliced lemon rounds, a three-tiered silver tray laden with savories, such as crustless sandwiches (bottom), scones (middle), and sweets (top). Ideally, you'll forego the tea bag for tea leaves and a strainer, and have several types of teas for your guest to choose from.

This set-up is prepared prior to the guest's arrival, as the hostess should never spend her time in the kitchen, but act as pourer.

Should the need arise for you to step away from the table, you may leave your napkin on your seat. To signal the end of your gathering, place your napkin, loosely, to the left of your plate.

Should you wish your guest to leave permanently and violently, leave a bomb under said napkin, so that it can't be seen prior to setting it off: by remote control, of course.

True, an explosive is messier than a poison, but the upside is that there is less of the body to dispose of—and it gives you the perfect excuse to redecorate!

"You brought Mary here, even though you know there's some assassin running around this mausoleum, waiting to take a pot shot at the man who invited her to tea?" Seeing Mary seated with Asimov, Jack can't believe his eyes or ears.

But yep, she's right there, for all the world to see. Realizing this is his chance to get the egg—in this case a taco shell—off his face, Asimov has invited the media to watch him play nice with an eighth grader.

I don't know what's in the satchel Mary lugged with her to the tea, but something tells me she didn't get the memo that she's supposed to be a star-struck acolyte.

I nod to Jack. "Believe me, this wasn't my idea."

"Oh yeah? Whose was it? No, let me guess. Daddy Dearest, trying to score brownie points."

I open my mouth to say something, but nothing comes out because he's right.

"If it's any consolation, she thinks Carl's a sell-out, and a douche."

"Interesting. All that, and she only spent a few minutes with the guy. Good to know she's smarter than her mother."

"You've already established how you feel about me, Jack." I'm able to keep my tears from rolling down my cheeks. He blurs before my eyes, in more ways than one. What right has he to be jealous, when he admits he can't commit to me, even if I were free of Carl? All it merits from me is a shrug. "Well, believe what you want. The truth is I did not invite Carl into the shower."

"Let's say I believe you. Once he was all over you, did you at least try to put up a struggle?"

"You know I did!"

Okay, not at first. But yes, eventually.

Like most fibbers, my first inclination is to glance away. Right now, I keep my eyes firmly on Jack. He's got to believe me.

He blinks first.

That's a good sign.

At least, I think so, until he mutters, "First Breck, now Carl. Maybe I should move out of the bedroom so you can do your job properly."

"What the hell is that supposed to mean?"

"I'll be glad to tell you, Mrs. Stone. The confab I had with Jonah was about one thing: he asked me how I'd feel about you becoming his mistress whenever he's in town. To be honest, the term he used wasn't so eloquent. He asked me if you were a hot fuck, and if I'd allow him to find out for himself, he'd throw a lot of business my way."

I'm so angry that my heart is pounding a hundred times a

minute. "What did you tell him?"

"That you had a mind of your own and if you decided to have sex with him, I wouldn't stand in your way."

But of course. All in the line of duty.

We stand together, silently, as Mary gives Asimov a photo op that, I'm guessing, he'll always regret.

"President Asimov, I don't get it." Mary's tone is innocent, but I know her well enough to recognize the cat and mouse game she's playing. "How can a two-year sentence of hard labor be considered fair for students who are only seeking a corrupt-free election, in Russia's so-called democracy?"

Asimov frowns at her audacity. "Mary, my dear, the people voted. That makes Russia a democracy. And there is a law in Russia against hooliganism." He leans forward. "In fact, what you and your classmates did to me this morning might have earned you the same sentence."

Mary folds her hands in her lap. "I enjoy free speech. You're making me happy I don't live in Russia."

Anger flashes in Asimov's eyes. Through his attempt at a smile, he murmurs, "I want to make it clear that the sentence they received was not issued from me, but from Russia's courts."

Mary smiles back at him. "But according to Russian law, you have the power to commute all sentences. Isn't that so?"

His pause is too long. Finally, he shrugs. "I have given it some thought, and I will continue to do so."

"That means a lot, to so many of us. Two million so far, and counting!" Mary lugs her heavy satchel onto the table, opens it and pulls out a ream of paper. "Here are our signatures. Young people all over the world, just like me, believe you'll do the right thing! Right now, you have our trust. And trust is what makes a statesman great. Don't you agree, President Asimov? But if your own people can't trust you to provide a fair election process, why should those attending this summit believe you when you say you'll quit making Weapons of Mass Destruction?"

As she reaches out to shake his hand, he is hit between the eyes with the obvious: Mary has him over a barrel.

At least one Stone has the nerve to speak her mind.

She's an inspiration to me. I grab Jack by the hand. "Jack, I told you I'm divorcing Carl, and I meant it. In fact, a process server hit him with the summons this morning. He may not like it—for that matter, Ryan may not like it, either, because he'll feel it will jeopardize the mission—but I can't go on pretending."

He starts to say something, but stops himself. I'm hurt by the sadness in his eyes.

"Donna, if you divorce Carl, you do it for you, and you alone. What we have—it will prove itself over time."

Time. The one commodity assassins never have enough of.

We both know this.

If this is his out, so be it.

I'm divorcing Carl no matter what. And now that Jack has made it clear I have no future with him, I've got nothing.

Wrong. I have my job.

And it weren't for the men in my life, I wouldn't be where I am today.

Someday I'll point this out to them.

Most likely in a dark alley, where they'll have no place to hide.

"Your daughter has put our honored guest's visit into a tailspin," Jonas Breck murmurs to me just as our dessert, strawberry dumplings, is being served.

Up until now, he'd been ignoring me, despite having me seated to his right during our sumptuous dinner. Instead, he's been trading asides with the South Korean defense minister, leaving me to swap pleasantries with some third-world dictator cursed with bad breath from an abscessed tooth. When this Idi Amin wannabe mentions he's having oral surgery here in Los Angeles, I wonder if he'll balk at the price tag. Then I remember he personally pockets all the aid money the United States sends his country. That should more than cover the bill.

Asimov sits to Babette's right, and Jack to her left. Carl stands against the wall, directly behind Asimov. Three others in his security detail are covering doors that go in and out of the grand dining salon.

One servant may not yet know it, but he's certainly on Carl's radar. He hesitates every time he serves Asimov. Just now, when Asimov declared he'll be tossing every activist in Russia into his country's newest state-of-the-art prison ("It's like your Gitmo, but with an arctic ambiance as opposed to a tropical one," he proclaimed with a laugh), the butler, a surfer blond dude with a slacker tan and obviously not well-trained in wait staff etiquette, lost what little cool he possessed and dropped a champagne glass on the marble floor.

When it shattered, all eyes turned toward him.

Carl's nod to one of his goons does not bode well for the boy.

When Carl is not watching the comings and goings of the servants, he glares at me. I'm sure he's angry about the divorce papers, but too bad. I just hope Bulldog doesn't become the very first name on Hilldale Police Department's Missing Persons roster.

Between Carl's steady gaze and my proximity to Breck, any appetite I may have had for anything, let alone strawberry dumplings, is long gone.

Still, if Breck supposes his statement will get a rise out of me, he's wrong. Instead, I give him a pleased smile. "Mary is not afraid to stand up for herself, or for others. I'm very proud of her."

"Your daughter is naïve about the world. In countries like Asimov's, if a girl doesn't fall into line and do as she's told, she'll be put into prison, where they'll break her spirit." He examines his hand as he flexes it. "Albeit, the pretty ones like her are sold to someone who can do so without harming the charms of their flesh. It's an interesting process. I've seen it done firsthand."

"Sex slavery is 'interesting?' I can think of better descriptions: Vile. Sick. Reprehensible. And that's just off the top of my head."

Breck laughs. "I hope you show more discretion than Mary in broaching that particular topic with Asimov. It's one of his country's greatest exports." He shrugs. "There's big bucks to be had in flesh peddling. Granted, it's time consuming, but one can imagine the sense of accomplishment one has when successfully forcing someone to bend to your will, not only without a struggle, but obediently. Even eagerly."

"You talk about it as if it's an equestrian sport."

"A perfect analogy, my dear Donna. With the right whip, and bit in her mouth..." He gazes at me, intently. "Has anyone ever told you what a pretty little mouth you have? It looks so... pliable."

That wipes the smile off my face.

"Mary reminds me of you: so proud, so sure of herself." He leans in close. "Her mouth is pretty, too."

If I were to kill him right now, the Brecks's sterling silver cutlery would give me several weapons to choose from. Besides the dinner fork and the steak knife, we were also given chopsticks in honor of our Asian guests. But by the time the fog of rage has cleared my eyes, I have quit toying with the most ideal one of all: the lobster pick.

Breck doesn't know how close he came to being carved up at his own dinner table.

He smirks as he adds, "I can only hope Janie proves to be just as outspoken as your Mary. But she doesn't have much of a role model. Babette isn't as—I guess the term is 'feisty'—as you."

I lean back, as if assessing his slight toward his wife. "You have a beautiful wife who loves you. What more can a man want?"

"What men want most is what they can't have." I feel his hand in my lap. "And they'll go after it until they get it."

It's my turn to for a little under-the-table shenanigans. I take my stiletto heel and grind into his ankle, right above his $1,600 bespoke patent leather John Lobb derbies. "No pain, no gain, right?"

I've got to give him credit. He doesn't scream. In fact, he's actually smiling, albeit gritting his teeth. "So glad to see you're into a little rough stuff. We'll make quite a pair." He points down to the other end of the table, where Jack is sitting to Babette's left. Tonight Asimov has the guest of honor seat, on her left. "I wonder if Jack will think the same of Babette."

Hearing Jack's name coming out of Breck's mouth makes me blush. Involuntarily I shift my leg, releasing him from my heel. "Jack thinks well of her."

"I'm not asking if he 'thinks well of her.'" His laugh is deep and hearty, as if I'd divulged the most clever bit of gossip. "I'm curious of what he'll think when he fucks her. I know firsthand— and others have confirmed it—she takes a while to warm up. But once she does, it's anything goes."

When Jonah's implication sinks in, my stomach tangles into a knot. Jack... with Babette? He didn't mention the second half of his conversation with Beck.

How convenient for him.

My eyes shift toward the two of them. Babette is leaning in toward Jack. He's speaking intensely. She gazes up at him, enthralled.

Suddenly, it dawns on me. I was the chum in the tide for her shark of a husband. While Jonah is occupied, she can stifle her boredom with Jack.

He'd go along with it, too, because it protects our mission. Something easier to do when you don't feel the guilt of a relationship.

I think I'm going to puke.

I've got to get out of here. I need fresh air.

As if reading my mind, Breck murmurs, "I can't join you now, but I'll be in my office at midnight, after my meeting with Asimov and his keeper." He looks up at Carl. "See that one, there? Asimov will rue the day he swam with that shark."

Just then, Carl looks over at us. I bat my lashes at him, before turning back to Breck. "Oh? How so, pray tell?"

Breck purses his lips, but says nothing. Obviously, he knows more about Carl than he's telling.

"Nighty night," I purr, as I rise to leave. "Oh, and by the way, don't wait up for me."

When the servants come to clear the table, will they notice the third-world dictator's lobster pick is missing? If so, and it ends up in Breck's corpse, he'll have a lot of explaining to do.

I've made my way over to Janie's room, to check on the girls. Abu is with them, showing them simple commands which, miraculously, has Eddie the Dog dancing, rolling over, and chasing his tail on cue, with lots of tail-wagging in between.

"Way to go!" I high-five Abu.

He bows his head modestly. "I owe you, Donna. That Nova documentary you suggested put me on the right track. I have to admit, the mutt and I have bonded. I'm going to miss him when this mission is over." His smile fades. "Speaking of which, the big cheese says kudos for your, er, diplomacy with Breck. With both of them, really, considering how the Missus is responding to you."

"You mean, how she's responding to Jack, don't you?" I keep my eyes on Eddie, as if watching him do flips will keep Abu from knowing my heart is breaking. "I've come to the conclusion that I'm the bait she put in front of her husband so that she can play footsie with Jack."

"If that's the case, I can honestly say I can't blame her." He lowers his voice, so that the girls can't hear him. "Janie's au pair, Antoinette, quit this morning without any notice. She'd been complaining to Babette about Breck's 'inappropriate attentions' toward her. That's not all. Every time Breck comes near Janie, she gets angry and clams up. The night before last, after he came into the room and berated her mother in front of her, the little girl wet her bed. She made Antoinette change the sheets quickly, and had her promise not to tell Trisha. She doesn't want to lose your daughter's friendship."

"Poor baby! Abu, do you think he's abusing her?"

"I... I can't say. But I do know he gets touchy-feely around her. And he had no qualms in groping the au pair in front of her. But when Janie told her mother and it was confirmed by Antoinette, Babette accused Antoinette of flirting with Jonah."

"Talk about denial!"

"You can say that again. For Antoinette, it was the final straw on the camel's back. As much as she loves Janie, she'd already heard rumors from the other servants about Breck's slap-and-tickle routine with Janie's previous au pairs. Oddly, though, she left a couple of things behind."

He walks over to Janie's bedside table, and opens a drawer. "See this crewel work? It's a scarf she was making for her mother's birthday. And she didn't take her library book. There will be a fee on it in another week. Also, she left behind her favorite sweater."

"Did you mention this to Babette?"

"No. But I did tell Edwina."

Since Asimov came to town, Edwina has been laying low, coordinating all the behind-the-scenes activities to make sure the summit runs smoothly.

"I guess the resignation of a babysitter isn't high on her list right now."

"On the contrary, she seemed quite concerned. Angry, in fact."

"Well, it does make more work for her."

"Oh, she wasn't angry at Antoinette. She's fed up with Breck. I'm sure she's been through this drill before, and she's tired of it. My guess is that she'll be the next to quit."

"He'd be lost without her. From what I can see, they have some sort of dysfunctional symbiotic relationship."

"You're telling me. I think she knows where the bodies are buried—literally."

That stops me short. "What do you mean by that?"

"She asked me into her office to pick up a print-out of the annual chart from Eddie's dog astrologer—hey, don't laugh! Trust me, you don't want to know what's in store for this poor mutt. Anyway, right as I walked in, Breck called her into his office and reamed her out. Something about a new transport company she'd hired losing a shipment from Moscow on the way to some private island. 'It wasn't perishable, was it?' she asked him, almost as a joke. He slapped her for it, said she knew it was, and that he'd dock her pay if it wasn't found. She didn't cry out, but she had his handprint on her face when she came back out."

Abu is right. Why would Edwina put up with such a vicious prick?

I kiss Trisha good night and walk out the door.

Lucky me, I'm walking past Breck's office just as his meeting with Asimov is breaking up. Three of the attendees—the North Korean defense minister, some Arab sheik who had seemed jealous of the attention Babette paid Jack at dinner, and Idi Amin Junior—give me knowing leers as they pass me in the hall. From what I can see, the only other person left in the office with Breck is Asimov and his ever-present shadow, Carl.

Just at that moment, the nervous young butler I remember from dinner scurries out of another hallway, and slams into me. The vodka bottle on his tray tilts precariously. I grab it before it falls, while he steadies the accompanying two tumbler glasses.

"Oh! Excuse me," he mumbles. "They... they called down, said to get this up here, while it's still chilled."

He shrugs helplessly and skedaddles, beating me to the reception alcove leading into Breck's office. Edwina, who must have been sitting at her desk in the corner, has risen to stop him. He freezes, as if he's seen a ghost.

"You can't enter until I inspect that," she admonishes him.

He looks frantic. "But... the kitchen said I'm to deliver it immediately—"

Her smile is calm, her tone soothing. "This will only take a moment."

She takes the vodka in hand and confirms the seal has not been broken. She then lifts the first glass to the light, and follows suit with the second.

"Smudges," she notes with a disapproving sigh. She takes a cloth from a drawer and wipes them thoroughly. The second time she holds them up to the light, she smiles.

"Perfect!" she proclaims as she hands them back to him.

He nods, picks up the tray again, and heads into Breck's office.

At that moment, Edwina looks up and sees me. Concern flashes in her eyes. Is it for me? Perhaps. She's fully aware of Breck's agenda for me.

Before I can raise a finger to my lips to quiet her, she calls out, "Sir, your midnight appointment is here."

I'm the lamb being led to the slaughter.

Asimov smirks at my appearance in the doorway. Carl's only acknowledgement is a blink of his eyes. When Breck walks around the desk and puts his hand low on my back—much too low—Carl gets it.

Only I take notice of the way in which he flexes his fists.

For once, I appreciate his jealousy. Or is it concern? I'm kidding myself. I know better.

"Ah! Just in time to join us for a good night cocktail! We're having a stellar vodka. It's a gift from President Asimov's special reserve."

He points to the bottle, which the butler is about to set down on the desk.

Apparently, being the center of attention is the last thing the butler wants. His hand shakes as he drops the tray onto the desk, causing the bottle to fall toward the floor.

Carl catches it, just before it hits the ground.

He looks up at the butler, whose face is drained of any blood.

Carl rises slowly with the bottle. He hands it to the butler. "Open it," he says.

The butler's eyes get large. Mutely, he nods and twists off the top.

Carl nods. "Now, pour some into a glass."

The butler's hands shake so hard that half of what he pours ends up onto the tray.

Carl picks up the glass, then holds it up to the light. Through a satisfied smile, he murmurs, "Thank you."

The butler heaves with relief.

He has almost reached the door when Carl says, "Now, drink it."

The butler stops cold. "I—I beg your pardon, sir?"

"I said drink it." He walks over to the man, glass in hand. "Here you go. Down the hatch."

For just a moment, the butler stares at it. There is no fear in his eyes, no resignation. Just surprise. He takes the glass, but pauses before sipping the clear spirits. After coughing down the last of it, he looks up with a shaky smile.

Then, choking, he clutches his chest and falls to the floor.

"What the hell!" Breck shouts.

Edwina comes running into the room. At the sight of the butler gasping his last breath, she screams and drops to her knees, sobbing.

Asimov, shocked, mutters something in Russian, which I am sure is some expletive. Then he turns to Carl. There's an angry exchange between the two men in the president's native tongue. Whatever Carl says to him seems to be calming him down. Carl calls into his headset, and within a moment, four more of Asimov's security detail are in the room. Two of them examine the body before carrying it away, while the others hover over Asimov.

"The vodka was poisoned." Carl may be stating the obvious, but his superiors still stare at him in disbelief.

When Breck finally speaks, his voice is actually trembling. "But... how? The bottle was sealed."

Carl shrugs. "I'm guessing the seal was broken, then resealed."

Breck shakes his head, still in awe that he skirted death.

I find it hard to believe the trembling butler was the Russian dissident we've been looking for. The telltale sign will be fingerprints, if they are on file anywhere.

In any event, I'm relieved Breck now has something to occupy his time. Slowly I back out of the room.

"Wait, madam," Carl commands me.

I laugh. "You're not serious, are you? You think I have something to do with this?"

"You were in the hallway with the butler prior to his entering the room. How do we know you didn't slip him the tainted bottle?"

"That is the stupidest thing I've ever heard!" I look from him, to Breck and back again. It doesn't help that now Breck is looking at me as if I've grown horns.

Well, screw him.

I mean, he can dream on, if he thinks I'm going to screw him!

Not that he'd want to, now that he thinks I almost killed him. Ha! If I wanted to kill him, it wouldn't be in front of witnesses. I'm too smart for that.

But, yeah, it would be as painful as a poison.

I'm still contemplating all the ways in which I could make him squeal like a piggy when it dawns on me.

Carl is really trying to pass me off as an accomplice to the killer.

Why, the nerve of that guy! If he thinks this is the way to stop me from divorcing him, he's got another thing coming.

I'm not afraid of staring him down. "Oh yeah? In this get-up, where would I hide the bottle?" My dress is too tight. They can all see that. At least, now they're looking above my neck, too. "Besides, if you check the security feed, you'll see I wasn't carrying anything."

Carl walks over to the computer on Breck's desk to do just that. He replays a few minutes of the video, freezing it when he gets to the moment the butler bumps into me. "Right there, you had a few moments in which to put a syringe through the seal."

"I told you, I'm not carrying a syringe. But if you care to search me..." I lift my arms. And yes, there is a smirk on my lips.

Carl frowns at my attempt at humor, then turns to Breck. "I'm sure your guest would like to clear up any questions which may arise about her proximity to this attempted assassination. I'll escort her to her room, where I can interview her more thoroughly."

Breck nods distractedly. I guess even he's not kinky enough to bed someone who could kill him.

If only I'd known this earlier, I could have shown him some of my handiwork. Wolverine, for example. Oh well, live and learn.

"So, you're going to 'interview me more thoroughly?'" Carl and I are almost at my bedroom door when finally I break the silence between us. "That has got to be one of the worst pick-up lines I've ever heard."

"Hey, you should be thanking me. Anyone else on Asimov's security team would be grilling you under a hot light, then renditioning you to Siberia for another little chitchat. And besides, it got you off Breck's radar for a while," he mutters. "By the way, it's not half as funny as your silly attempt to divorce me."

"It's not silly. I'm serious. It's time we part ways. I don't know if you've noticed, but we're not good together."

"Sorry, babe. I'm in it for the long haul. Till death do us part, remember? Besides, you'll have to catch me first."

"I did catch you! That is, I sic'ed Bulldog on you, and he served you."

"Oh, contraire, mon ami. From what I remember, I never touched the summons."

"Liar! I saw you, with my own eyes! And besides, that's the whole point in having him do it for me. He's a legal witness."

"Not any more, he isn't.'"

"You didn't... Oh, my God, Carl! Did you exterminate him?"

"Nah. He's still breathing... I hope." He pauses in thought. "How long can someone stay in the trunk of a car?"

"Depends. Did you drive him out to the desert and leave him there?"

"No. I had a couple of the boys leave him in East South Central. I figured someone would jack the car eventually, hear him screaming and let him out. Not that it's much of a car. The dude drives a Pinto. Who does that these days, anyway?"

We've reached my door. But no way will I unlock it and let Carl in. I make this clear by leaning against the knob.

He ignores the obvious and leans in over me, anyway. "Donna, I want you to know I was proud of Mary today. She gave it to that asshole, Asimov, right between the eyes. You've done a great job with her. With all three of them."

Hearing this brings a lump to my throat. I can't imagine being away from my children for five years, no matter what the circumstances. Carl's greed has cost him dearly.

I turn my head so that Carl can't see the tears glazing my eyes. Gently, he tilts my face up, so that he can look me in the eye. "Are you doing this for Jack? Did he ask you to marry him?"

The last thing I'll admit to Carl is that Jack dumped me the minute I told him about my plans. Instead, I say what I know is a blatant lie. "No. Jack has nothing to do with this."

"If you're being honest with me, I'm relieved. And not just because I have no doubt you'll take me back when you realize the big picture, but because he's not who you think he is."

"Really, Carl? Are you going to start playing mind games with me again? Don't bother, because I won't fall for it this time. And besides, you're the last person who should be trash-talking Jack."

"You're wrong. If anyone knows Jack Craig, it's me."

Just at that second, the door opens behind me, and I almost fall inside—

Into Jack's arms.

He's wrapped in a towel, and nothing else. He gives a wary squint when he sees I'm with Carl.

That doesn't stop Carl grabbing my arm, pulling me toward him, and giving me a deep, soulful kiss.

Caught as I am between the two men who know best how to thrill me and how to aggravate me, I decide to allow one a cheap thrill, and let the other be aggravated.

Serves them both right.

Tomorrow, I'll flip it on them. Or aggravate both of them. It depends on my mood, which, right this very moment, leans toward the latter.

But by the way Jack yanks me away from Carl and slams the door, I may be convinced to change my mind.

CHAPTER 14

GOING BACK FOR SECONDS

When you're a guest at someone's dinner table, it's always polite to leave a little something on your plate. Even if it's the best dish you've ever had. Even if you haven't eaten in days.

Even if it's the last meal before you face a firing squad.

Because the last thing you'd want your captors to remember about you was that you were uncouth!

"No make-up sex," I say to Jack with a pout. "I'm not in the mood."

Still, I reach back to unzip my dress, slowly...slowly...

Right about now, I'm guessing that Jack is also pining for a little forgive-and-forget foreplay. Afterward, we'll have the talk that is long overdue. The one about why, when I'm free of Carl, he's afraid to commit to me.

So, why does he stare at me, as if I've lost my mind? Worse yet, now he's laughing so hard, he doubled over.

I stop mid-zip. "What the hell is so funny?"

"You. Or I should say, your lousy sense of timing."

"My what?"

He dismisses me with a wave of his hand. "Abu, what do you think? Is Donna sometimes a day late and a dollar short?"

"Nope, I'd say she's right on time. This shindig was getting dull." Abu's voice comes from the farthest corner in the room.

Yep, he's there alright. To make matters worse, Arnie is sprawled over the chaise lounge. Both stare at me as if I'm a piece of prime rib.

Quickly, I pull up my zipper. Too quickly, unfortunately. The lining of my dress's gets stuck in its teeth. The more I tug, the worse it gets.

My frown, directed at Jack, only makes him laugh harder, until finally he steps behind me to take a look. Does he notice how I shiver when he touches the small of my back? When he zips it up, he does so at the speed in which I zipped it down.

What a tease.

It only makes me want him even more.

Not that I'll ever let him know that. I shift away from him so I can lean against the wall. "What is this, a slumber party?"

Noting my stance, Jack roams over to the bureau. He picks up a pair of his cufflinks and shakes them in his fist, like dice. "Nope, a strategy session. We need to regroup—and fast. Unfortunately, the butler whom Carl forced to drink the poison vodka was one of our guys."

I can't believe my ears. "What? That nervous guy was an Acme operative?"

Arnie nods forlornly. "He was Kirby Lonergan, from Tech Ops. For the past six hours, something has been blocking our shadow feed in Breck's office suite. Since I wasn't due to deliver flowers until late tonight, we had to send someone else in, to plant another bug. Kirby was the only one at Acme with cater-waiter experience. The tray he had was bugged. It was to be our new eyes and ears—at least, while Breck and Asimov were to be enjoying their after-dinner drink and conversation."

"He would have been better off with a little field op experience under his belt," I say. "The poor kid was as nervous as a hen in a den of foxes! You couldn't pull off one of your costume dramas?" Arnie's disguises are a thing of wonder.

Arnie shrugs. "Ryan didn't want to take the chance that the guardhouse's facial recognition system would rat me out."

"That's a shame, considering the confab that occurred there earlier tonight, not to mention the one taking place now."

Frustrated, I kick off my heels. Big mistake. Eddie snags one before it hits the carpet. Before Abu can grab him, he's under the bed with it.

"Damn it, Abu, that's a sixteen-hundred-dollar Louboutin! I thought you had that mutt under control!"

Abu grimaces. "Sorry, Donna, but it takes more than a forty-eight hour training session to undo two thousand generations of rat hunting."

"Quit whining about the shoes and tell us who was in that meeting," Jack growls.

"The North Korean defense minister was in there, along with that South African dictator who's been wiping out whole villages with his gangs of killer 'tweens. Also, there was the Arab playboy sheik who's got a crush on Babette."

I said this for Jack's benefit, but he ignores it. "Someone poisoned the vodka. We know that for sure. But if the butler didn't do it, who did?"

Arnie accesses the shadow security files through his iPad. Finally, he finds the one he's looking for. "It may have been Carl. He went down to the kitchen and handed it to Kirby right before the meeting began, and told him to wait for the call to bring it up, with just two glasses."

Jack turns to me. "Does that answer your question?"

I shrug. Yes, it does, but I'm not going to give him the satisfaction of knowing it. At least not now.

Jack smiles, as if he read my mind. "Arnie brought a camera with him. It's hidden inside a microdot. We have to get it in there and fast."

All eyes turn to me.

I shake my head adamantly. "Whoa, whoa, whoa! I just crawled out of that snake pit. Now you want me to sashay back in?"

Arnie gives his iPad screen a series of taps. "No one's in there now. I guess it's got too much dead dude mojo." His tone is that of a parent with a five-year-old.

"Besides, Breck is spooked by what Carl told him about you." Jack adds, "Which, I'm sure, plays to his benefit. If he can get rid of us, no one can stop him from assassinating Asimov and starting World War III."

"We've been through this. Carl said it to Ryan. Asimov is a Quorum ally. They won't harm a hair on his chinny chin chin."

Jack smirks. "He's lying. Imagine what a nuclear apocalypse would do to furthering the Quorum's cause."

I shake my head adamantly. "I believe him when he says he wants out. He misses his children. If he behaves himself here, he'll hold onto his Watch List clearance."

Jack shrugs. "He tells you exactly what you want to hear, Donna. You should know that by now. Besides, if the Quorum gets what it wants, he rules the school. He'll take the children, and you wouldn't be able to stop him. That is, if you wanted to."

"What the hell do you mean by that?"

"Do I have to spell it out? You're falling for his bullshit. But what's new about that?"

"Ouch! Mommy and Daddy are fighting." Abu sighs mightily. "I guess the party really is over." He motions for Arnie to follow him out the door.

"Wait a sec.... And"—Arnie swipes a few screens—"we're in the clear. For the next twenty minutes, the security cameras will see empty halls between here and Breck's office." He tosses me a ring. "It's behind the gem. Ideally, you'll place the microdot somewhere on the desk. But it's got to be on something that won't be moved. Ryan wants me to emphasize, if Breck walks in on you—well, we know you can take care of yourself."

I nod. I know the drill.

And so does Jack.

Despite this, he turns his back to me. He'd rather stare out the window than think about me with Breck.

He's not the only one.

If he said even one word to stop me, I wouldn't walk out the door.

Oh, who am I kidding? As much as I hate this part of my job, it has to be done.

By the time I get back, Jack will have reconciled his jealousy with the reality of this dire situation.

And finally, we'll kiss and make up.

Does make-up sex feel so great because of all the anger and hurt that came before it? I think so. I hope so.

If I'm right, whatever happens in Breck's office will have been worth it.

The conundrum I face is simple: where does one hide a black microdot on a glass desk, which holds nothing at all? Even underneath the desk, it would stand out like a speck of dust that should be whisked away.

The ultimate goal: hide in plain sight, preferably on a surface where no one will see it, let alone touch it.

The John Singer Sargent painting.

I hop onto the large, wide credenza, to examine it more closely. Sargent captured the debutante's wide-eyed innocence, but her sly smile betrays any presumption of decorum.

The black microdot disappears on the surface of her glossy patent leather slippers.

It is not a Louboutin.

"Bad girl! You fucked up, royally."

The declaration, low and menacing, comes from behind me.

It's Breck.

I brace myself to face him—

A hard smack, followed by a woman's cry, comes from the office's reception alcove. "Mr. Breck, please! There was no way I could have anticipated—"

"That's not good enough, Edwina. I pay you well to anticipate everything."

I hear a scuffle, then a thud against the wall between the rooms. Just in time, I roll off the credenza and crawl behind one of the four large white leather couches that make up the room's conversation pit. Breck holds Edwina around the waist with one arm and drags her over to his glass desk. Once he has her back pinned against it, he is able to rip open her blouse and shove his hand down her bra. Her left breast pops out. He looks down at it, admiringly. "Small, but adequate," he murmurs before putting it in his mouth.

At first Edwina is too stunned to fight him off. But the feel of his lips on her nipple rouses her out of her shock. She grabs hold of his hair and yanks his head away from her chest.

He yelps, then reaches for his hairline. "You bitch! You pulled out my plugs!"

He cracks her across the face with the back of his hand. The force of his slap hurls her onto the floor. At first she lays there, stunned, but then she stumbles onto her hands and knees. When she shakes her head, the blood trickling from her nose drops onto the white carpet. With a trembling hand, she reaches up to cover it, but too late. Breck sees it, too.

He steps on the hand covering the blood. "Fucking whore! If that stain doesn't come out, I'm docking the cost of a new carpet from your salary."

Her painful cry only makes him laugh. Then the abusive prick jerks her up by her hair and slams her into the wall, right next to the Seurat. He pins her down with one hand while he undoes his belt with the other.

"No... please..." She whimpers. "I'm... You can't... We shouldn't..."

As if he'll listen. She grimaces as he positions himself into her. She screams with the first stab.

"You're tight. That's good!" His words come out in grunts between his rhythmic humping. "But you're too loud, my dear." When he covers her mouth with his hand, her eyes open wide.

Can she breathe?

One way to find out: I pick up a heavy metal ashtray. In a second, I'm standing behind him. If I hit him just right, his skull will crack open, just like an eggshell—

Edwina sees me. Her eyes open even wider, if that is possible. She shakes her head No.

It's against everything my gut tells me is the right thing to do: kill the son of a bitch. And yet, I hesitate.

Because the woman he's raping in front of me is begging me to leave them alone.

Walking away would save me from being reprimanded for an unsanctioned hit.

It would save our mission, too.

And so I nod back, and walk away, disgusted at Breck. And at myself, too, for buying into Edwina's irrational need to put up with him.

Just as I make it to the doorway, Breck groans, spent. So much for fifty shades of Breck. More like fifty seconds.

The satisfaction in his voice curdles my blood. "My God, Edwina, you're bleeding? Well, what do you know, a thirty-year-old virgin! Who'd have thought it. You need to get out more, live a little. After the summit, why don't you take some time off? Maybe you'd like to join me on my private island."

I slip down the hall before I change my mind and kill the son of a bitch.

I awaken to the sound of someone crying. Only when I hear Jack whisper, "It's okay, Donna. I'm right here for you..." do I realize it's me.

As we lay in bed together, he holds me as if he'll never let me go.

After the hell I've seen, this is my heaven.

"Do you want to talk about it?" He strokes my back gently. He isn't asking me to relive the horror of Edwina's rape. He saw it for himself. The moment I activated the microdot, the camera hidden inside caught it all, in living color, for those monitoring it to see: not just Jack, but Ryan and Arnie, too.

By the time I got back to the room, Jack had already texted Ryan his recommendation that I be pulled from the mission: not for what it might do to me, but for what I might do to Jonah Breck, to the detriment of the mission.

Ryan texted back RECOMMENDATION DENIED.

When Jack showed it to me, I threw the cell phone up against the wall. "So much for safety in the workplace."

Then I showered and stumbled into bed.

In my nightmares, I was Edwina, pinned to that wall.

And there was nothing I could do about it.

Now that I'm fully awake, I realize the metaphor, even if I don't appreciate the irony.

My whisper is so soft that I don't know if Jack hears me. "I can't get her—her total submission to him—out of my mind."

"You gave her the opportunity to stop him. She decided not to take it. Please Donna, don't blame yourself for that."

I turn to face him. I can't see him in the dark, but that's okay. His scent—a pungent essence of talcum and sweat and strength—is the reality I crave in my surreal existence. His features are etched deeply in my fondest memories, my fiercest fantasies, and the prayers for my future.

His gentle kisses on my brow don't surprise me, nor does the touch of his finger, which wipes the tears from my cheeks. He may not believe this, but I yearn to have him inside of me. This desire is not born out of lust, but the need for comfort. When I seek him out with firm practiced hand, he whispers, "We don't have to do this now."

"I want to, Jack. I need to have you with me, this way."

I build him up and guide him into me. This act of love takes place on our sides. No one dominates. No one is subjugated. Each of us takes with awe and appreciation what is given and received with an open heart. With each thrust, we moan together.

Until we come, in unison. The explosion is hot and furious and silent, except for the gasps of bliss that escape too soon for two people for whom every moment of life is precious.

Now nothing evil or cruel can force its way into my soul.

When we are done and he has fallen back asleep, it strikes me that our response to this incident brought us back together, even closer than before.

But we'll be torn apart again when the inevitable happens: when we have to pretend to be what we aren't, a couple.

No more.

I'm through playing house. I want a real husband, and a real life.

Chapter 15

Seating Arrangements

When devising your seating chart, always keep your favored guests close at hand! If the guest is male, he is to be seated on your right, whereas an honored female guest will be seated to the right of your spouse.

Should you find the delicate hand of your female guest of honor in the lap of your spouse, resist the urge to pour scalding soup down her décolletage, or to cut her jugular with the steak knife. Doing so only serves to ensure a death penalty. Too many witnesses, so little time!

Instead, excuse yourself between the main and dessert courses in order to cut the brake line in her car. The timing is believable, and it's a quick fix to an odious problem, especially if you're serving something as complicated as Baked Alaska or Crepes Suzette. (Again, resist the instinct to toss anything flaming in your guest of honor's lap. Payback is sweeter when brake fluid is involved.)

Just before eight o'clock, I wake to find I'm alone in bed. Jack, who has to pretend be at Breck's beck and call, must be out on the golf course with our host.

If Breck is lucky, he won't be left alone with Jack.

Or with me, for that matter. Despite what Ryan says, accidents do happen.

I sigh when I hear a rap at my door. I pray it's not Carl.

When I crack it open, I find Edwina standing there. She cleans up nicely. No bruises, no red-rimmed eyes.

But the moment our gazes cross, she looks away. Still, I have to ask, "Why?"

She smiles for the cameras. Then, for the benefit of anyone listening in, her voice is cheery as she asks, "May I come in?"

Of course I move aside so she can enter.

If only it were that easy to get into someone's head.

Edwina stands by the window, staring out onto the wide expanse of verdant lawn. I'm patient, busying myself with the task of pouring tea from the breakfast cart. Jack must have requested it for us before he took off.

When I hand her a cup, the tremor in her hand causes it to

rattle in its saucer. I touch her wrist gently.

"You must think I'm a fool." Her whisper has the gale force of a lost soul.

I shake my head. "I think you were scared. And overpowered by him. I don't mean just... physically." It's my turn to look away. "He's got money. He buys power from everyone. I get it. You felt helpless."

There is no joy in her laugh. "No, you're wrong. I knew that, eventually, he'd take me. And I wanted it."

She stops when she sees the horrified look in my eye. "Please, don't look at me as if I'm some pathetic fool because I mean what I say. You see, it's the only way I can—"

Her eyes opened wide at the realization that she may have said too much. "Let's just say that we have a symbiotic relationship. He depends on me, and I want to keep it that way. So it works... for now."

"How did you meet?"

Her eyes narrow. "He's an old family friend." She sips the last of her tea, then sets the cup on the coffee table. "I've come to ask a favor. Really, the request is Mr. Breck's."

Seeing my frown, she quickly adds, "No, it's... it's nothing like that. In fact, he has moved on to—well, let's just say, his attention span is fleeting."

Good to know, since my trigger finger is itchy. I shrug. "What does he want?"

"Perhaps you can join Mrs. Breck on her shopping engagement, and then for quick lunch prior to the ballet. Her personal shopper is... she is indisposed."

I can only imagine how, and with whom.

"You see, today is Mrs. Breck's birthday. I've also arranged for lunch at Il Fornaio. Once there, you'll be taken into a private room, where Mrs. Breck's new friends will surprise her. Won't that be fun?" Edwina wraps her arms together, as if a chill just came over her. "While she's out, I'll be coordinating the set-up for her surprise party: a circus! The event planner will deliver the tent the moment Mrs. Breck's driver, Robert, signals us that you are far enough down the road. After dinner, the Brecks will take a stroll around the grounds. We'll all be waiting for them in the gardens below the house. By the way, her new friends are invited to the party as well."

She smiles through her pain, and through mine, too. Penelope and the gang? Well, there goes my appetite.

"Mrs. Breck will presume you've arranged the lunch. Mr. Breck would prefer that. I hope you don't mind, Mrs. Stone."

"Of course not." What else can I say? To tell the truth to someone whose whole existence is based on a complete lie would be a waste of breath. "It seems you've thought of everything, Edwina."

"I'm sure I've forgotten something." A shadow of a smile darkens her lips. "Nobody is perfect. Then again, if that were the case, neither of us would be here and praying we were anywhere else, now would we? The driver will ring for you, promptly at ten thirty."

"I think I'm falling in love with your husband."

It's on the tip of my tongue to ask, Which one? But that would be silly. Of course, I know Babette is speaking about Jack. No doubt about it, Carl also exudes an animal magnetism, but five minutes alone with him and you'll see immediately that he's an acquired taste.

You'd have to be a glutton for terrorism.

My gaze shifts from the Cavalli frock in my hand to Babette's center reflection in the three-way mirror, where she holds a Michael Kors crepe gown with a fishtail hem against her. "I can't say that I blame you. It's an easy thing to do."

"He is truly kind." She doesn't look up at me. Instead, she shakes her head, as if the thought is something she finds hard to fathom. "He came into the nursery the other day, to check on Trisha. The way in which she jumps into his arms! If only Janie..." Her voice trails off.

When she looks at me, there are tears in her eyes. "We're enrolling Janie in a boarding school."

"But why? I thought the whole point of building Lion's Lair and settling in Hilldale was so that she could stay home with you."

"I want that more than anything in the world! But now, with Jonah's pending appointment, we feel Switzerland is a happy medium."

"Switzerland? That's on the other side of the world!"

"Yes, but it is closer to Russia than Hilldale. And that's where

Jonah will be based when he's appointed the U.S. Ambassador to Russia. The president will be making that announcement tomorrow, when he arrives at the summit."

Jonah Breck is taking an ambassadorship?

"It's a stepping stone. International diplomacy looks good on a curricula vitae when you're being groomed for the presidency." She laughs at my look of shock. Really, it's one of horror, but she doesn't know me well enough yet to figure that out. "He's bored. He knows he can buy presidents. Now he's out to prove he can buy the presidency." Suddenly, she's distracted by a shiny gown the color of soft peaches. She plucks it from the rack and holds up to examine it. "What do you think? Does the color make me look pale?"

Not as pale as I look now, I'm sure. "It's just perfect. Babette, what will happen with Edwina? I presume she'll be out of a job."

"Not at all! She's part of the deal. He can't do without her. Anyone can see that. Besides, she grew up in Russia. Her fluency in the language was one of the reasons he took her on. Well, that, and he'd never say no to any request Asimov makes."

"Asimov recommended her?"

"Yes. He knew her mother. Poor thing passed, last year in fact."

Interesting. Why would Edwina lie and claim that Breck was 'an old family friend?'

As far as Jonah Breck running for president someday, ewww yuck!

"Babette, what will happen to Jonah's investments in all those green start-ups? Will he have to sell them off?"

"No, not at all. Believe me, he's got that covered. It will be part of our blind trust. He's turning Breck Global Industries over to someone who will ensure it stays on course. In fact, his hand-picked successor is here for the summit. "

"You mean Rutherford Collins, BGI's chief operating officer?"

Babette's nose wrinkles in disgust. "Heavens, no! That sniveling little fool? Jonah keeps him around as a joke. He's letting go of him right after the announcement is made."

"Then I presume you mean Garret Conover, your attorney."

"No, Garret will be taking a leave of absence from his firm in order to join Jonah as his chief attaché at the U.S. Embassy in Moscow." Her eyes light up. She enjoys the game she's set up. "The new CEO is one of the men in Asimov's entourage. You know the one: he's tall, dark, and very handsome. I'm laughing because it's so obvious he has taken notice of you."

Carl.

Carl will be running Breck Global Industries?

Something about this stinks to high heaven.

I have to get back to Lion's Lair, or at least lose Babette long enough to use my cell phone and tell Jack and Ryan this news.

I don't know what to say so I simply smile at her, all sweetness and light. "That's such a pretty gown! Why don't you try it on?"

Babette glances down at her elegant jewel-encrusted Patek Philippe watch. "Do I have time? Aren't the other women going to be angry if we show up too late?"

"You know about your surprise luncheon?"

"But of course! And the circus, too." She puts a finger to her lips. "Nothing much gets by me. I have my spies everywhere. But let's keep it our little secret, shall we? I like the fact that everyone assumes I'm clueless. Makes it easier, all the way around."

She looks down at the dress in her hand. "I'll take it anyway. No need to try it on. That's what my personal shopper, Marilyn, is for—when she's not too busy fucking my husband. It's another reason I hope Jonah actually makes it to the White House: maybe then he'll be too busy to screw the help. Although that's probably wishful thinking." She sighs. "Speaking of help... do you think your foreign exchange student would be open to considering an au pair position with Janie, until her new school begins? Since Antoinette took off, we're in a bit of a bind... Oh, Inga has no work permit? What a shame! Well, no harm in asking..."

Penelope and her acolytes are in the middle of singing Happy Birthday to Babette when my cell phone rings, much too loudly. Caller ID shows that it isn't Jack. This is a major disappointment. I've been dialing him every five minutes since Babette gave me the news about Breck. Now that I know Breck's end game–the presidency–it makes sense that he's trying to look as statesmanlike as possible. Pretending to play peacemaker between the two great (or at least, two of the three most heavily armed) nations on the planet will certainly impress voters.

Ha! If only they knew his position on women's rights. Infidelity is second nature to him, and rape is an afterthought. Let's face it. He's a poster boy for men who should be castrated.

At the very least, he's certainly lost my vote.

Should he make it as far as his party's primary, I'm sure the security footage of Edwina's rape will be invaluable to the competing party's candidate.

Despite the fact that, once again, I've been placed all the way in the back of the private dining room with the rest of those who have found themselves on Penelope's personal Watch List, the club's fearless leader can hear my cell phone's ring tone: Gaston, from Beauty and the Beast.

Oh no, it's Alan. I guess I'm about to find out Bulldog's fate.

Penelope's eyes narrow with the intensity of a lethal laser beam set on search-and-destroy. In no time at all, she has honed in on the culprit: me. She jerks her thumb toward the door as she mouths the words OUT OF HERE, NOW...

For good? Forever?

Ah, if only...

In order to speak in private, I bury myself in the cloak closet before connecting with this lifeline. Even before I can utter a word, Alan lets loose with a string of expletives that would bring tears to an army sergeant.

When, finally, I can put my cell phone near my ear, I answer in the sweetest voice possible: "Good morning to you, too, Alan."

"Do you know what your husband did to Bulldog? The poor dude is in a Psych ward again, he's so traumatized!"

"What do you mean, again? Has this happened before?"

"Believe it or not, he doesn't do well in the trunks of cars. Reminds him of the solitary confinement he endured in his last marriage."

"Oh... kay. Hmmmm. Please apologize for me."

"I'll do more than that. His medical expenses are going on your bill."

"Lovely. Thanks for the heads up." What else can I say? I'm a desperate woman. Babette's tidbit about Carl taking over Breck Global Industries has made it even more crucial that I keep him away from my kids and me.

"Listen, Alan, you have to send someone else to serve Carl, like, immediately."

"That may be difficult. The word is out that your man is violent, not to mention connected."

"Whatever happened to all your 'Booyah' crap? I'm counting on you! Do whatever it takes, Alan. Double the server's fee, if you have to."

There's a pause at the other end of the connection. Is he thinking, or did some shiny object fly by the window and distract him? With Alan, you never know.

Finally, he exhales a thought. "I'll send in my best man, the Panther."

"I thought Bulldog was your best man."

"He was—until your psycho hubby broke him."

"Yeah, Carl is a real charmer. Tell the Panther he can find Carl at the Hilldale Performing Arts Center this afternoon at two o'clock, during the Kiev Ballet's performance of Swan Lake. Most likely he'll be backstage, or in the VIP box with his client. Hey, just out of curiosity, Alan, why are all your process servers named after animals?"

"Ha! Have you ever eaten with one? Trust me, it's like feeding time at the zoo. You have to watch your fingers when you reach for the bread basket."

I click off before that vision takes hold. Il Fornaio's pasta primavera is to die for, and I'd like to hold onto my appetite, thank you very much.

Once again, I dial Jack, but my call rolls into his voice mail. As a last ditch effort, I try Emma.

"Wow, perfect timing! I was just about to call you." Emma's voice sounds a bit shaky. "Not about the mission, but...well, something's wrong in the neighborhood."

This stops me cold. "What do you mean?"

"I've been to the park a couple times, you know, when Aunt Phyllis has asked me to walk your dogs Lassie and Rin Tin Tin, or to call Jeff in for dinner. I've gotten friendly with the au pairs and nannies. They keep their ears to the ground in the homes they work in, so they always have a lot of gossip. Turns out that one of the nannies caught the kid she sits for looking at a porn site, and guess who was on it?"

"In our 'hood? With all the lonely, horny housewives, it could be anyone."

"Nope, it wasn't one of those light erotica slap-and-tickle housewife sites. This one is called Island of Misfit Sluts, and its claim to fame is the fact that the women aren't there by choice. They are being broken in as quote-unquote sex slaves. Talk about fifty shades of sick! Really, it's thirty days, not shades—the initiation period, I mean. This brings viewers back to watch how it happens. Last week's sex slave was Antoinette!"

"Are you sure the girls aren't paid to act innocent and submissive?"

"No way! Antoinette really is—that is, she was an innocent girl. I've already checked out the site with the FBI's Internet Division. They've been tracking Misfit Sluts for at least two years. Many of the slaves are under-age, as young as ten! Both the FBI and Scotland Yard have been trying to find the source of the feed to the server, but it's offshore and it's got an air-tight shield around it."

Curiouser and curiouser. Not to mention sicker and sicker. "Your intel certainly validates Abu's contention that she left unwillingly. But the big question is with whom? Everyone has been in lockdown during the summit."

I sigh. The thought of women of any age being held against their will has my stomach churning.

"An even bigger question is how? Acme's satellite surveillance has been tracking all cars going in and out of Lion's Lair," Emma continues. "Thus far we've got nothing. And here's something really scary: a few of the au pairs have been approached about taking her place. The Brecks' representative, that creepy Collins dude, is offering twice the going salary."

"Any takers?"

"In fact, the Coxheads' nanny, Serena La Costa, is considering it. She desperately needs the money."

"I know the woman. Tall, with long dark hair. Very young. She's, what, about twenty?"

"Yep, that's the one. From Venezuela. She was in college here, to get a teaching degree. But had to drop out to send money home to help support of her family."

"I guess her student visa has expired then."

"You're right. She's hoping to score a green card. That cruel Tiffy Coxhead is working her to the bone with the promise of helping her get one. How did you know?"

"It's the same M.O. as Antoinette." I sigh and shake my head. "Listen, Emma, I don't think what I'm going to ask next has anything to do with Antoinette's disappearance, but I need you to do me a favor and scan INTERPOL for information on Edwina Doyle. Use whatever you find. Fingerprints and facial profiling, too. Something about her just doesn't fit."

"What do you mean?"

"Once, when I asked her why she puts up with Breck's shenanigans, she mentioned that she owed him her life. She also claims he's an old family friend. And yet, when I asked Babette about Edwina just now, she insists Breck hadn't met Edwina until just before he hired her, and that he did so based on Asimov's recommendation. One of them is lying, and my dollar is on Edwina."

"Hmmmm. Until I get something back, a quick way to actually follow her movements is to use this new gel Arnie is testing. You squirt it on the surface of a pair of glasses, and it sends a visual of whatever the wearer is looking at. Edwina wears glasses, right?"

"Yes! That would be ideal! Will he be doing a flower run today at Lion's Lair anytime soon?"

"Let me ask."

A moment later, Emma comes back on the line.

"Unfortunately, he did it this morning."

"Wait! I've got the perfect cover for him. Breck is putting on a circus tonight, for Babette's birthday. Can he crash it?"

Emma must have covered the phone with her hand, but I can still hear Arnie shout "Yahoo!"

I can't help but smile. "I take it he's up for the gig."

"Frankly, I don't think you could have kept him away! He's pulling up the schematic now, from the party planner's iPad. He suggests you rendezvous with him in front of the House of Mirrors."

"How will I know him?"

"He'll be the clown with the green hair and the plaid shoes. You can't miss him."

"Great. Tell him we should meet prior to the cake being cut. Say, nine o'clock."

"Will do, boss lady."

"Hey, speaking about bosses, is Ryan around? I have to speak to him."

"Sure, I'll connect you."

The next thing I hear is Ryan's growl. "Speak."

Ah, always a man of few words. And he wonders why he's still single.

"I thought you should know that Breck is up for the ambassadorship to Russia. According to Babette, it will be announced tomorrow, when POTUS is at Lion's Lair."

"Heard it already. Our client called this morning with the

news."

"Oh, really? And did our client also mention whom would be taking control of Breck Global Industries?"

"Yes." This time Ryan's brevity is shorthand for something I already know. Unless Carl is the indisputable initiator, we can't touch a hair on his head.

I'm almost afraid to ask, but I have to. "Have you mentioned this to Jack?"

"I thought I'd leave that to you."

"Coward."

"You got that right. Try to break it to him gently."

We both know that's easier said than done.

I hang up to find that Babette's surprise luncheon has already broken up, and a crowd has gathered around the cloakroom door. I have to get out of there if we're going to make it to the ballet in time, but that won't happen anytime soon if these women don't get their wraps first.

In other words, I'm stuck in the Eighth Circle of Hell. Dante calls it Fraud, but I know it to be Procrastination. None of these women wants to get back to housework, carpool, or kids.

Someone yells above the din of gossip. "Hey, hand me the beige lamb's wool cape, will you?" She tosses me a ticket with a number on it.

For real? Seriously, how many cloakroom attendees can afford Marc Jacobs.

Oh. My. God. There's a five-dollar bill underneath the ticket. Score!

I find the right coat and hand it over. The tickets and bills keep coming.

Like I said, sometimes it pays to be in the Eighth Circle of Hell, especially if your credit card bills include pricey couture, like Marc Jacobs.

CHAPTER 16

WHEN THE WRONG PARTNERS FILL YOUR DANCE CARD

Balls and cotillions are such fun—when you're with the right one!

True, a gorgeous gown and your adroitness at scintillating conversation will make you the belle of the ball, but frustrations can arise when an annoying waltz partner fills your dance card even before the first chord is struck.

Solution: spike his punch with eye drops, then have him twirl you around the dance floor. In time, he'll be running to the loo in order to spew his guts for the duration of the evening, and you'll be free to dance with pithier swains.

"That's bullshit! What's the world coming to?"

Jack's angry declaration has several of the ballet's patrons turning around to shush him into silence. Granted, the prima ballerina's pirouette dipped a bit, but it's not the end of the world.

I waited until the closing scene of Swan Lake to break the news to Jack about Carl's new gig. In hindsight, bad move.

We're sitting with Babette, Janie and Trisha, in a private box. Jack's eyes, which had been following ballet's prima ballerina in her death throes, narrowed and move toward Carl, across the orchestra loge. He's sitting behind Breck and Asimov, in another box. The three of them have been ignoring the performance. Instead, they've been talking in low voices.

"So, he gets full immunity from our government—and a trillion dollar company to run?" Jack's whisper comes with a shake of his head. "This means the Quorum may be controlling the next president of the United States!"

I raise his hand to my lips, and brush it with a kiss. "Believe me, it will never happen."

The final scene is over, and the audience is on their feet. The applause is deafening. The tears streaming down the prima ballerina's face causes her make-up to run.

Trisha pulls my hand so that I can hear her exclaim through her own tears, "Mommy, she is so bee-you-ti-ful! I'm so happy to be a ballerina, too."

This is what every mother lives for: the wonderment she sees in her child's eyes, a rarity in this jaded, mixed up world.

As promised, Asimov has arranged for Janie and Trisha's ballet class to go backstage. I've arranged for the Panther to be there, too. Not to my surprise, the Panther is underwhelming: a little old man who's claim to fame is that he's so unobtrusive that no one even realizes he's there.

Not even Carl, who doesn't see him as he sidles up next to him. I hold my breath as the Panther slides an envelope out from under his jacket. He reaches up to tap Carl on the shoulder.

But just then, the Kiev Ballet manager shouts something in Russian as he points to one of the ballerinas—the one who played the Black Swan, in fact—who is running up the aisle, to the back of the theater. She flings open the swinging double doors and, with a flying leap, bounds beyond them.

But no! Suddenly, she falls.

Carl has shot her.

Not that any of the little girls or their mothers know this. His gun has a silencer, and the ballet's fawning fans are too busy ooohing and ahhing at the Corps de Ballet in their pretty tutus.

The next time the doors swing open, I spot two of Asimov's men dragging the prima ballerina's limp body down the hall.

Angrily, I run over to Carl. "What the heck did you just do?"

"She was sent here to kill Asimov. She failed, and I shot her before she could get away."

"Oh! So she was from the Russian dissident cell?"

He shrugs. "Apparently so."

"You're lying." Jack pushes Carl, as if daring my soon-to-be ex to prove him wrong. "Tell her the truth. The manager yelled out that she's an asset who was attempting to defect."

Carl shrugs. "I forgot that Lover Boy here speaks fluent Russian."

I turn to Carl. "How dare you? She had a right to leave! And to shoot a gun in a theater filled with innocent bystanders, not to mention children. It's reprehensible!"

"She picked the wrong time and place. Asimov doesn't need another public relations debacle, despite what she thought to the contrary."

"You mean, like the one Mary, our daughter, caused?" I'm glad he winces when I point that out. "Now you can pretend we're three for three: that there are no more assassins on Asimov's tail. Fine with me! The sooner you call it quits and move on, the better for all of us."

"I told you, I'm here to stay, so get used to it."

"Oh yeah? That's what you think." I look around for the Panther. Where did the little bastard go?

Then I notice him: passed out, at Carl's feet.

Nope, not passed out, but dead. His eyes are open, and the summons is still in his hand.

I guess seeing Carl draw his gun scared him to death.

He wasn't a panther. He was a scaredy cat.

I can't wait to hear what Alan has to say about this. Probably that Carl will never be served. That I'm stuck with him, forever.

We'll see about that.

When Carl turns back toward Asimov, I take the summons from the Panther's cold, stiff hand, and slip it into my purse. Then I force my lips into a smile and tap Carl's shoulder. "I hear congratulations are in order, that you're going legit. Gee, I guess you really impressed Breck."

I'd like to slap Carl's knowing grin off his face. "Yeah, well, he recognizes talent when he sees it. I'll be bringing home a lot of bacon, so I hope you have your pan ready."

It's ready, all right. In fact, it's All-Clad: a twelve-inch five-ply stainless steel and aluminum skillet with a copper core. If I smack his head in just the right spot, he'll be joining the Panther on that big firing range in the sky.

Ah, well. A girl can dream, can't she?

Truth is, I take just as much fun in plotting Carl's legal exit from my life as I do when fantasizing about his fare-thee-well. "So, what say we celebrate your promotion? Dinner is on me. Do you remember the Sand Dollar? It was once a favorite of yours."

We celebrated many a special occasion there. Well, he'll remember this very last time, too.

"You're on. But won't lover boy over there be jealous?"

He nods toward Jack, who grins back, but shoots him a bird nonetheless.

Carl's smirk is aimed at me. "Oh yeah, I forgot! Your fella has other plans. While Asimov preps for POTUS, Jack is joining Breck and some of the delegates on another night out on the town... What Jack didn't tell you? Where do you think he was last night, after he left you? Not to mention the night before that. Breck knows some hot strip clubs."

Carl can read it on my face: the hurt. And yes, maybe just a wee bit of jealousy.

Jack sees it, too. His nod is so subtle that I barely catch it.

Yeah, I get it. All in the line of duty.

Sorry, no. It doesn't make me feel any better.

I gulp in order to keep my voice from shaking. "I know the score. And, by the way, so does Jack. If you're set on hanging around for a while, we're all going to have to learn to get along, right? So, what do you say? Will I see you at Sand Dollar, down at the beach, say sevenish?"

"Sure, okay. Works for me."

He leans down and pats Trisha's head. "See you around, little one. A lot, I hope."

Um... NO.

Trisha must be thinking the same thing. As he walks off, she sticks her tongue out at him.

Wish I could do that too, but it would set a bad precedent, as would cutting the jerk's jugular, so I also resist the urge to pull out my stiletto and go Ginsu on his ass. Monkey see, monkey do.

Being a good mom takes a modicum of restraint.

Jack and I drive back to Lion's Lair in silence. I wait until we're alone in our room to ask the obvious.

"So, why didn't you tell me where you were going?"

Jack winces at the question. But I think his nervous tic is his fear of what I'll do with the nail file in my hand. Thus far, I've just been sawing away at my half-ass home manicure.

"What with this whole issue with Carl resurfacing, and you wanting to divorce him so that we can marry, I didn't feel the timing was right to mention that being in Jonah Breck's good graces means hitting every titty bar and whorehouse in the county."

"You've been hitting whorehouses, too?"

Jack is quite aware that now I'm holding the nail file in my fist, like a knife. It's not exactly an SOG, but it'll do the trick, which is why he backs away, slowly. "You know what they say. 'In for a dime, in for a dollar.'"

His feeble attempt at a laugh dies when he sees me stab the file into my gel eye mask. Oops! The gel squirts onto Jack's tuxedo.

I click my tongue. "My bad."

"Donna, cut me some slack! As soon as Asimov leaves, we're out of here, too, and good riddance. I never thought I'd admit this, but I've seen enough tits and ass to last me a lifetime."

"Oh, now I get it! Now you want me to walk around in a burka, is that it?" I look down at my breasts. To make my point, I cup them, then turn in his direction. "Are you implying that Pixie and Dixie aren't 'perky' enough for you?" I turn, so that he can look at my backside. "You know, just last week you told me this thang was Gaga-licious."

"I don't think those were my exact words."

At my stage of life, furrowing a brow is the last thing a woman should do. Still, his counter merits due consideration. "Perhaps your exact words were that you could 'eat off my posterior.'"

"Exactly. Seriously, you took that as a compliment?"

He ducks just in time. A flurry of feathers takes flight when the nail file stabs the pillow where his head once was.

"Donna, no surprise here, but you're taking what I've said out of context. Breck is a creep. He chooses them young, and he treats them rough. Twice, the house madam had to go into his room with a bouncer. The dude is a sadistic whoremonger. Although I have to tell you, Carl comes in a close second." He shakes his head in disgust.

"I couldn't care less about Carl! My question was about you. Really, us. I guess what you're telling me is that you haven't... that you haven't..."

"Exactly. I haven't. I pay the ladies what they're owed, then listen to them bitch about their boyfriends. From what I gather, it's hard out there for a 'ho." He rewards me with a naughty leer. "That said, if you want to walk around the house in a G-string, pasties, and high heels, I'm all for it, although, I don't know how the kids would take to it. There's an 'ew yuck' factor when it's your mom who's parading around like a—"

"I would never walk around the house like that! Our bedroom... maybe. If you wanted me to."

To prove that he does, slowly, gently, and with practiced hands, he strips me of everything.

Except for my heels.

His gaze takes me in, top to toe. Admiration, lust,

anticipation, it's all there.

As he pulls me down onto him, I murmur in his ear, "Maybe we can buy the house next door, and give it to the kids as a gift. Then I could walk around naked all day... and so could you."

"I'll call the bank on Monday, to arrange for a loan."

"Ha! As if we'd qualify!"

Even as I say it, I wish I'd bitten my tongue instead. Man, talk about a cock-blocking mood killer!

But not for long.

And yes, the heels have a lot to do with that.

Chapter 17

Cocktails before Dinner

Yes, cocktails before your evening meal are a must! Not only does appointing one of your guests as a bartender make for useful busywork while you put the finishing touches on your meal, it loosens tongues for vibrant conversation around the table.

A word of caution: resist the urge to serve sweet, frothy or frozen drinks, which may ruin the appetite. Stick to martinis— preferably dirty, most certainly gin—which allows for a complimentary flavor to your appetizers, and ensures a healthy appetite.

Here's a great little tip: If a guest gets sloppy and crass, the taste of a knock-out drug such as Rohypnol won't be noticed if the right olives (Spanish Queen green, pitted and stuffed with nothing; I repeat, nothing) are part of the drink. Cheers!

I get to the Sand Dollar a few minutes early. I've already reserved what used to be our favorite table: out on the deck, next to the rail, where the waves from the Pacific crash up against the rocks below.

I also make sure we'll be served by my favorite waitress, Anna. She is fast, discreet, and knows what Jack and I like to order. No doubt she'll raise a brow at seeing me with Carl, since he was before her time. She need not worry. Her excellent service will be duly rewarded.

And one way or another, tonight Carl will be served with his summons.

I'll be left with the tab, but it will be worth it.

I'm already seated. The martini in front of me is gin, dirty, and shaken.

My hands are shaking, too. I blame it on Carl, who has suddenly appeared on the deck. The first place his eyes go are to this table.

Ah! So he hasn't forgotten it, or us as we were so long ago.

He can't hide the look of longing he has for me. As for me, I have to blink back my tears for our loss. My smile is hardened by the resolve that it is time to move on. I've worn a soft cashmere boatneck sweater, better to show off the heart-shaped pendant necklace he gave me so long ago. I'm hoping he remembers it, and that it softens his resistance to my request that we go our separate ways.

But then it is wiped completely off my face when he takes my outstretched welcoming hand to pull me out of my chair and into his arms.

Is it the heart, the soul, or the mind that remembers the feel of every kiss? Perhaps all three play a role in my memory. I can just imagine the heart pumping out the desire that makes me ache for it, while the mind reminds me of all the reasons why it is so wrong to want to feel his lips on mine again.

But it is the soul that is scarred with the footprints of our mutual journey. It starts with a cautious dance of shared attraction. Then the race to passion. The waltz of true love and commitment. The sure and steady walk down the aisle of matrimony, where we promised to love and cherish, until death do us part.

Until Carl's death.

For five and a half years beyond that hideous, glorious day when he was presumed dead and Trisha came into the world, I believed he'd been an honorable man.

Stunned by his miraculous return to life, I believed every word of his supposed mission to save the world.

Until I found my dead neighbor in her freezer, where Carl left her to die.

When, finally, he admitted the truth—that he'd resurfaced in order set off a nanobomb at the same nationally televised Little League event where the Democrat's nominated candidate for president was tossing out the first ball, and oh, by the way where our son was to pitch—the blinders came off fast.

My soul now knows our paths need not cross any longer.

This is why I am divorcing him.

Later, if push comes to shove, I'll kill him, too.

As for this bittersweet kiss, let him think what he will. I get to ruin his appetite later: both for me, and for the bloody steak he'll order.

Call it just desserts.

"Thanks for inviting me," he says, as he pulls back from the kiss. "Ah! You're wearing the necklace I gave you."

"In memory of all the good times." Does he hear the regret in my voice? I can't help it. The truth may hurt, but it sets us free. "Shall we order?"

I've kept the conversation light through our shared appetizer of oysters on the half shell, and our main courses of surf (mine) and turf (his). We've also moved from martinis to white wine. This way, I've got a fifty-fifty chance he'll be too drunk to shoot me, should he decide the easiest way to get the kids is to knock me off first.

Don't think I haven't thought of doing the same to him.

To keep things civil, I've been dropping tidbits I know he truly hungers for: any news about our children. "Trisha loves ballet. I'm so glad Babette was able to secure the tickets to Swan Lake."

"In truth, you should thank Asimov for that," he says with a shrug. "It pays to have friends in very high places."

Asimov, a friend? Try an enemy—of the state. I know this

hasn't been proven yet, but there's still time, so I let that slide. For now, anyway. "Jeff has turned out to be a serious athlete. But he's frustrated that every other guy on his basketball team is taller. I keep reminding him that there's a good reason his coach chose him to be the team's center. He's the highest scorer on the team."

"That kid! He's amazing." Carl's smile is wistful. "Is there a fall baseball league here?"

I nod. "Yep. And he plays in it, too."

"Is he strengthening his pitching arm?" Carl lettered on his high school baseball team and got a college athletic scholarship because he was such a great pitcher.

"Fabulous. He's always first on the mound." I hesitate, then add as nonchalantly as possible, "Jack has worked with him on his two-seam fastball, and his curve ball. He's better with the former than the latter."

Carl shrugs. "Well, Jack can step aside, now that I'm back in town. Oh, and he can move out of my house, too."

I drop my fork gently on my plate. Has he noticed my knife has disappeared from the table? I hope not, because I may have a better use for it than cutting my scampi. Right now, it's hiding in the right sleeve of my cashmere dress. In the meantime, I have to bide my time. "Have you noticed how tall Mary has gotten since—?"

How do I put this delicately? I can't just come out and say since that time you tried to blow all of Los Angeles, including your family, off the map.

I finish the sentence with a smile. "I mean, since the last time you saw her?"

"Yes, she's grown into quite a beautiful young lady. Not to mention how outspoken she is." Even as he smiles, his eyes narrow. "I'm guessing she gets that from my side of the family. We all know her demure sensibility comes from you."

I click my wine glass with his. Good of him to play nice.

"Is Mary dating anyone?"

I chuckle at this absurdity. "Oh, no! She's too young to date. She's not even thirteen yet!"

"Ha! Thought so. She's got the wool pulled firmly over your eyes."

He pulls out his smart phone and hits a few digits. What comes up is an audio file notated as Mary's Boyfriend Stepping out of Line.

"What the hell, Carl? You mean to tell me you've been monitoring our daughter's phone? That's an invasion of her privacy!"

"Okay, then, I'll delete it."

He reaches to press a button, but I stop his hand. "Well, since it's already done."

I'd like to smack that satisfied smile off his face. Instead, I sit motionless while he presses another button on his cell phone. The next voice I hear is that of Trevor, Mary's latest crush: "So, like, while your mom and dad are at this big party, can me and some of the guys come over and play Spin the Bottle with you and Babs and Wendy? I swear, nothing below second base."

What the hell?

I scramble for my purse and my sweater. "Put the rest of my

meal in a doggy bag, and take it back to Breck's joint! I've got to get home, like, yesterday—"

"Whoa, whoa! Calm down." He pats my hand gently. "It's all taken care of."

"What do you mean by that? Oh my God! Carl, tell me you didn't eliminate him?"

"No, of course not. I just thought I'd teach him a lesson. Or two." He leans back. "Let me put it this way. The kid won't be kissing our daughter anytime soon, but he can still use his teeth to eat."

I rise to leave, but he grabs my wrist. "Donna, I'm joking. I texted his mom a copy of the audio file—anonymously, of course. Because she's another Hilldale helicopter mom who's afraid of what others will think of him, I'm sure she was mortified. He'll be in lockdown for at least a month. Heck, for all I know, after what she just heard she may keep him on a tight leash until he's twenty." He pours more wine in my glass. "You can thank me later. I know how."

"Ain't gonna happen, Carl." I gulp down my wine in one long swallow. "Look, I know you've had your fun with the process servers, but it's time to face facts: I no longer want to be married to you. Forget that you deserted me five years ago. Forget your 'occupation—'"

"You mean our occupation, don't you?"

"Yes. Guilty as charged." I fling my napkin onto my plate. "We may do the same job, but here's the difference between you and me. First, I work my career around my kids, not the other way around. And second—and this is a very big point, Carl, so listen up—I'm one of the good guys. I'm not scheming with despots and dictators to take over legitimate governments. I'm not selling WMDs on the black market. And I'm certainly not blackmailing heads of state with the threat of nuclear war."

"Everyone is a bad guy, Donna. Every politician, every head of state, every corporate baron, and every righteous jerk who wants to cram his cause down the rest of our throats. Frankly, I enjoy tweaking their noses and taking their lunch money." To my shock, he has the audacity to lean in and tweak my nose. "Speaking of self-righteous know-it-alls, enlighten me. When you snuff out a target, does an angel get its wings? I don't think so. And yet, you don't hesitate to sneer at your neighbors."

At that remark, a few heads turn our way. "Keep your voice down!" I hiss at him.

He ignores me. "Like I was saying, you sneer at your neighbors because they stab each other in the back. Well, at least they don't use real knives."

He jerks my arm straight down. The knife drops out of my sleeve and clatters when it hits the floor.

Once again, the other patrons look up from their dinners and frown at us.

I smile and wave. Show's over. "That's it, Carl. I'm out of here." I tap Anna on her arm as she passes. "Can you bring our check, please?"

She nods, and walks off.

"What's your end game with Breck, Carl? Don't leave me in suspense. I know you're dying to tell me."

"If I do, I'll have to kill you."

198

I'm laughing so hard now that others are staring. "Since when do you need an excuse?"

"You're right. I don't. Because when the time comes, there will be no way you can stop me." The smug bastard takes a sip of his wine. "As for Breck, I love new experiences. Lucky me, I just happened to be the right guy in the right place, at the right time. I've impressed him with my security skills."

"What a joke! Those two kills were mine, remember?"

"Yeah, but Breck doesn't know this, and he's the only one who counts. To him, you're just a lonely, frigid housewife."

"Frigid? Did that bastard actually come out and say that?"

"Yep. Sad, isn't it? Considering how much you pride yourself on your femme fatale rep." He shakes his head. "Don't take it personally. Frankly, I applaud you for avoiding that horndog as long as you have. Trust me, he's one sick bastard."

"I know. Jack has already warned me."

He frowns when he hears Jack's name. Well too bad.

"Seriously, Carl, since when do you care what he does to me, or any other woman, for that matter? I know the Quorum will take full advantage of his ambassadorship in Russia."

"My sweet, naïve, little wifey! Don't you get it? The ambassadorship is a stepping stone. The big prize is the presidency of the United States. With what it takes to buy an election these days, Jonah Stanford Breck IV is the perfect guy to help us do it. When he does, he'll remember who his friends are. And right now, he and I are bosom buddies."

He leans back, satisfied he's put me in my place.

Out of the corner of my eye, I see Anna walking over to us. Now it's my turn to burst his bubble.

In her hand is a tri-fold pamphlet, which she hands to Carl. "It's been a pleasure serving you," she says, smiling sweetly.

He opens it and shakes it, but the bill doesn't fall out as he expected. Stymied, he looks carefully at the pamphlet.

It takes him a few seconds to realize what he's staring at are his divorce papers.

Anna has already disappeared into the kitchen.

"Don't worry, Carl. I've already taken care of the bill. I told you dinner was on me, didn't I?" Noticing a couple at a neighboring table still staring at us, I say loudly, "Yes, sadly we're getting a divorce! Thank you for witnessing this. Anna is a wonderful 'server,' isn't she?"

Embarrassed, everyone turns away from us.

"Touché, Donna." I wish his voice didn't sound so ominous. He stands up. "May I?" He indicates he wants to pull out my chair. When I stand up slowly, he takes my jacket and holds it out for me.

Maybe he can be civil about this after all.

As if.

The moment my arms are in the jacket, he shoves me over the deck rail.

But just in time, I grab onto it with one hand. Three stories below us, waves smack the rocks with such ferocity that its tangy sprays are tossed rail high. In no time at all, my new Kate Spades are soaked.

"Damn it, Carl! Pull me up! Right now!"

"Not until you agree to give me full custody of the kids."

"What? Are you crazy? Over my dead body!"

"Sure, what ev." I feel his heel on my knuckles. He crouches down. I guess now that the fun and games are over, he's going to help me up.

But no. He's grabbing at my throat, for my necklace.

"Just a little something to remember you by," he whispers.

To hell with that.

To keep him from snatching it, I push as far away from the rail as possible, but between the pain of his foot on my hand and my tired arm, I can't hold this position for very long.

I've got nowhere to go but down.

Thank goodness it's high tide.

Before I hit the water, I have one thing to say to him. "Face it, Carl, you have commitment issues!"

My words echo off the cliffs. Just as I slice into the surf, I'm sure I hear him laughing at me.

Aw, hell. I'm wearing cashmere.

CHAPTER 18

KILLING THE LIFE OF ANY PARTY

There is always that one guest who seeks to grab all the attention, one way or another. Maybe it's through grand declarations or pithy bon mots. Maybe it's with slick dance moves. Maybe it has to do with the fact he's taken your favorite lampshade and turned it into a sporty chapeau, providing petite amusement for those who revel in his tipsiness.

If in fact it is the third route your party animal chooses, be prepared to spill a drink on him while he unscrews the lamp's finial from its harp. If you're lucky, the shock he receives will knock him unconscious. That way, you can shove him in a corner and claim he's in his cups as well as your lampshade. Let the party begin!

It takes me about a half-hour to drive back to Lion's Lair. The butler who answers the door doesn't like the fact that I'm sopping wet. Too bad. To appease him, I hand him my waterlogged shoes and make my way to my room barefoot.

Jack is in the room when I get there. "What the hell happened to you?"

I imagine my grin resembles the Cheshire cat, albeit a half drowned one. "Carl was officially served his divorce papers, in front of witnesses."

He shrugs. "Oh yeah? You better check the obituary page tomorrow, to see if your server made it through the night."

"You sound sooooo happy for us. Don't you see? It's the only obstacle standing between us and marriage."

"I'm just being honest." He unbuttons my wet cashmere top. "I thought we agreed that we don't need to be married to be 'us.'"

I move away from him, toward the closet. I pretend to be perusing a selection of dresses, but in reality, I'm trying hard not to cry. "Spoken like a guy with cold feet. I told Carl he was afraid of commitment. I was wrong. Carl is at least committed to being close. It's you, Jack, who has commitment issues."

"No, you don't get it. I am committed to you—to us. But Donna..." He stops, for what seem like a lifetime.

His, and mine.

Ours.

Then, "Donna, I can't marry you. Not now, anyway."

He waits for that to sink in, for me to turn around, to acknowledge him some way.

To accept this.

But I can't.

In truth, I won't.

Giving up, he heads to the door. "I love you, Donna. I always will."

I hear the door close behind him.

Sobbing, I drop to the floor on my knees. It's time for a good cry. But no, I've got to force myself to stand up. I must save myself from this pain.

Why is loving someone with all your heart so much harder than saving the world?

True to her word, Babette acts completely surprised when Jonah walks her down to the lower gardens, where the Big Tent has been set up. She blushes on cue at the sight of jugglers, clowns, acrobats, tightrope walkers, and the sword swallowers who are already entertaining the guests: all of whom turn, on cue, to shout Happy Birthday to a woman who could pass for half her age.

This beautiful woman should be enough for her husband, but no. His carnal appetite is insatiable.

They both know it.

Babette is married to a monster. And now that he's got his eye on the White House, her hope that he buries his puerile tendencies may finally be realized. She may not be able to keep him in line, but his political handlers will.

Or, perhaps the Quorum, since it has the most to gain and the most to lose.

I walk over to Trisha and Janie, who are hanging with Abu and Eddie. The dog sits obediently at his mistress's side, watching her every move. He remains calm despite all the ruckus on the lawn in front of him.

I give Abu a thumbs-up. "I can't believe it! You've gotten Eddie to chill out completely."

"Best yet, he's a pretty decent attack dog. Even Janie knows the command. I figure that, with her nanny situation being a revolving door, she needs all the protection she can get."

"Let's hope she never has to use it."

We click champagne glasses to toast his wish.

Then we follow the girls down the hill to the makeshift boardwalk, where the sideshow has begun in earnest.

For the past hour, I've been hanging with the girls and enjoying myself. The carnival acts have been wonderful. So far, Trisha's favorite is a bearded lady. I don't have the heart to tell her it's a man in a dress.

Like the rest of Lion's Lair, nothing here is as it seems.

Worse yet, everyone has something to hide.

The girls' innocence is bliss. As for me, it's almost time to turn back into a pumpkin.

It's a few minutes to nine, which means Arnie will be here any moment now. I scan the crowd for him but catch sight of Edwina instead. She frowns as she glances around for someone: the birthday girl, I assume, since it's time to cut the seven-tier birthday cake.

Edwina spots Babette exactly when I do. She and her most revered guest, President Asimov, are strolling the grounds.

They've just reached a large tent topped with a sign proclaiming HOUSE OF MIRRORS. The two of them chat and laugh while Breck trails behind. He keeps looking at his watch. Out of the corner of my eye, I see Rutherford Collins walking toward him. With him is a young woman: a young, pretty brunette. Where have I seen her before?

Then it hits me: It's Serena, the Coxhead's au pair.

I shake my head in disgust. So, Collins talked her into the job after all! Well, the joke's on him. If he's looking for major brownie points from Breck, he's too late.

Thick within the crowd is another person of interest: a green-haired clown with plaid shoes, walking with purpose toward the House of Mirrors. Aw heck, Arnie's got the worst timing in the world! The last thing I need is Breck watching the drop.

I head down the hill, but it's already too late. Arnie hightails it into the tent, just as Babette and Asimov get there, with Breck right behind them. Breck has turned on the charm. He's stroking Serena's arm. When she pulls away, he whispers something in her ear. Whatever it is causes her to nod reluctantly. She allows him to lead her into the tent.

Like a lamb to slaughter.

Collins knows the drill. Three's a crowd. He takes off, with a smirk on his face.

Our paths cross on my way down the hill. "Having a good time, Mrs. Stone?"

After what I've just seen, I'd like to punch him out. Instead, I dimple up and bat my eyes. "But of course! I have to say, that snake charmer is pretty scary."

Little does he know I'm referring to his boss.

The House of Mirrors lives up to its name. I'm reflected on every wall. Some of the mirrors are angled or distorted so that I look more svelte than I really am, while others scare me into thinking I better get on a diet, pronto.

The eerie lighting casts large shadows on all surfaces, making it hard for my eyes to adjust to the room's true shape, let alone to see where I'm to go from here. Ominous music and cackling laughter, coming in over a sound system and bouncing off the mirrored walls, are just as disorienting.

In fact, there are several hallways to choose from. I'm guessing that most people take the middle one, or the one on the right. Arnie being the contrarian he is, would have gone left, so I do, too.

Oddly, the mirrors are angled in such a way you can see everyone else walking through as well. They don't seem to see you, however. And when you reach out to touch them, you hit a mirror instead.

Even the ceiling is mirrored. It reminds me of Cloud Gate, the art installation in Chicago, which also has a concave surface, much like a human navel, as well as omphalas: reflections of the same image, several times over, in various places on its curved surface.

In one mirror, Babette and Asimov are walking down a hallway, laughing and talking. In another, Breck strolls with Serena. She looks terrified. Who can blame her? Having Breck hold your hand is scary enough in broad daylight, let alone in a spook house. Having separated from Babette and Asimov, he places an arm around her waist and pulls her close. She's struggling, but no matter how hard she pushes him away, he is much too strong for her.

My first thought it so break them up, but just then, Arnie appears in the curved ceiling mirror. I wave at him, but he can't see me. Obviously, he's roaming down another hallway. To hell with this covert crap. I take my cell phone and dial his number. The other noises drown out the ring tone he's known for—the Star Wars theme—but I hear him through my receiver:

"Hey! Where are you?"

"I saw you enter, so I followed you. Why didn't you stay out front?"

"I forgot if we said we'd meet inside or out. Then I saw Babette and Asimov coming toward me, and I freaked! I thought I should keep moving. But now I'm lost."

"Look up at the ceiling."

I can see through the curved ceiling mirror that he's doing as I asked. "Now look to your right...do you see me?"

The mirror's surface must be backward, because it looks as if he's turned left instead. Finally, he catches my reflection, too, and waves back. "Okay, Donna, what do we do now?"

"Just stay there, and I'll walk toward you."

The next thing I know, there are gunshots, then shouts.

All the lights go out, except for the track lighting along the floor.

I pull the Walther PPK I've braced beneath my jacket at the base of my spine, and get into a tactical stance. I look up at the mirrored ceiling to see who I can spot, and where. The moan I hear came from Asimov. The mirror around the Russian president has shattered, and he's bleeding. Was he shot, or was he speared by flying glass shards? It's hard to tell, but he's certainly shaken, and it doesn't help that Babette is bawling and screaming, as if it's the end of the world.

Where the hell are they?

I'm moving through the hallway now: very slowly, very carefully—

I see it: in one of the distorted mirrors: a figure, crouching, gun in hand. I take aim and fire, but the assassin's gun goes off first. The victim lets loose with a bone-chilling cry, then a stream of curses.

The voice isn't Asimov's but Breck's. Apparently, the assassin has shot the wrong person.

Couldn't have happened to a sweeter guy.

At the same time, my own bullet hits its mark. There is a loud groan, but also the sound of someone running away.

I dash to the spot where they were hit. There I find a bullet casing from the shooter's gun. There is also blood, so at least I wounded the son of a bitch.

I look up at the ceiling mirror in time to see the dark figure stumble through an outside exit.

As I turn the bend, I run smack into Breck and Serena. He is on the floor, still cursing and groaning. On the other hand, she was smart enough to wrap her scarf around his wound, as a tourniquet.

Before I run after the assassin, I toss her my phone. "Hit the first button. When my husband picks up, tell him to track via the cell phone's GPS where you are, and to bring help!"

I don't wait to hear her response, but rush on down the hallway.

I find Babette and Asimov a moment later. His face has cuts from the flying glass. Other than that, he is fine.

Babette grabs my arm. "Did the shooter hurt anyone else?"

"Your husband. He got shot in the thigh, but he'll be okay. Stay here with President Asimov. Help is already on the way."

The news leaves her in shock. She's almost swallowed her fist. Babette Breck is living proof that love is not only blind, but deaf, dumb, and forgiving.

I can hear the harried footsteps of Asimov's security team. I know I've got to find Arnie so that he can complete the drop and get out of there.

I look up at the mirrored ceiling, to scout for him—

And run smack dab into him.

He's so happy to see me that he hugs me, almost choking me. "Thank goodness! Here!" He tosses me a small jar. "Remember: a little dab will do you. Just the outside of the lens."

"Got it! Now, follow me out."

We run down the hallway, but it's too late: the security team is coming in the back entrance, too.

I pull Arnie with me, behind one of the mirrors. "It's now or never. Slide out under one of the panels of the tent."

"I can do that?"

"It's canvas, silly! Do you really have to ask?"

He crouches and rolls. I can hear his floppy shoes scrambling away.

I slip my gun back into the holster.

And just in time, too. Both Carl and Jack converge on me at the same time, from different directions.

Carl seems surprised to see me. I stick my tongue out at him. Yes, I am invincible. Get used to it, dude.

"I winged whoever it was, but I didn't see him," I say, even as I ignore Jack's admiring thumbs up. "Asimov has a few cuts from broken mirror shards. But Breck took a bullet in the thigh. He'll need a doctor, pronto."

Carl eyes me suspiciously. "Not from you, I hope."

I shrug. "While it was tempting, no."

Jack pulls out his cell and punches out a number, Edwina's, I'm presuming.

When, finally, she picks up, he explains the situation.

"Edwina is up at the house," he relays back. "She's calling Breck's personal physician. He'll be here within a half hour. In the meantime, security will get everyone to the house. If the shooter is hurt or bleeding, he should be easy enough to find. Unless he's already off the property somehow. For all we know, it's someone who slipped in when the circus came to town."

What if they find Arnie? I don't know how he'll fake his way out of it. That has me worried.

"This will fuck things up royally," Carl mutters.

If he means POTUS will probably blow off the summit, he's right. But I'm guessing his remark has to do with some bigger scheme in play.

Until I find out what it is, I'll play stupid, which isn't too far from the truth. "Aw, gee! Then I guess the party is over." I make a pouty face. "Don't be so glum, Carl. The way you guys were going at it, I'm sure every pole dancer between the OC and LA will be happy to have a night off. If you get lonely, there's always the bearded lady. When she's in your lap, you barely notice the five-o'clock shadow."

For once, I leave him speechless.

Perhaps he's seriously contemplating it. He did say he was into new experiences, so maybe he'll go for it.

CHAPTER 19

JUST DESSERTS

A dessert party is a wonderful way to get everyone together for a late night event, without going through the hassle of creating a full meal for them. Be ingenious in what you serve. And remember: variety is both the sugar and spice of life!

That said, consider a pie, a cake, and cookies. But don't stop there! "Wet" desserts, like a flan, pudding, ice cream or sorbet, satisfy the palate after your guests have feasted on your groaning board of flour-based fare.

Fruit is also a great addition to your table, especially for those who proclaim loudly and proudly that they're on a diet. Yeah, right. Such party poopers! To test this theory, place an éclair made with dark Belgian chocolate right in front of them, and tell them you promise it will keep their weight in check.

You don't have to mention that it is laced with a time-release laxative, too.

"How much longer do we have to wait here?" Penelope asks imperiously.

She has every right to be upset. For the past two hours, Carl and his security Nazis are still sorting out everyone's whereabouts while the shooting took place. It's a slow process, since they have to match every one of the three hundred party guests with the footage from the moment of the shooting prior to hustling them out the door.

"Who cares! It's a par*tay*!" Hayley whoops. "Don't be such a tight-ash shtick-in-the-mud. I mean a stick-in-the-mush... Ah, hell, you know what I mean!" Easy for her to say. Or not. She's been slurring her words all night. Par for the course for someone who's polished off a whole bottle of Armand de Brignac by herself.

Her breath is sparklingly sour enough to make both Penelope and Tiffy take two steps away from her. Penelope shrugs. "For once, she's right. Let's just make the most of it. Besides, if we hang here long enough, maybe we'll get to see President Asimov one more time before he leaves."

I wish Penelope and the rest of her momtourage would shut their yaps for a few minutes, so I can focus on the news coming in from Emma Central on my earpiece. Emma is giving me a play-by-play of what is being discussed in Breck's bedroom while he's being stitched up by his doctor.

Apparently, Breck is screaming. Not because he's in pain, but because POTUS is cancelling his appearance at the summit.

In response, Breck has threatened to end the summit. The Secretary of State tells him his attitude is irresponsible, and that it would be a breach of diplomacy.

"Oh...wow!" Emma squeals in my ear. "Breck just told the Secretary of State that he can take the ambassadorship and shove it up POTUS's—"

"—I couldn't care less about Asimov, Penelope! Or the Brecks, for that matter," Tiffy sniffs. "Donna, you owe me an au pair. That exchange student of yours will do quite nicely."

"What?" I look over at her. "Just what in heck are you babbling about?"

"I've lost Serena—to the Brecks, of all people! They've offered her twice what I can pay her, to watch after that little brat of theirs." She pulls out a compact to check her lipstick. "This morning, Breck's people came and got her things. Just like that! She gave me absolutely no notice at all. No two weeks, no nothing!"

"You're telling me Serena quit?"

"Duh! Are you losing your hearing, or do you have ADD? Nothing to be ashamed of. It runs in the best of families... at least that's what the doctor tells us, as it pertains to little Logan. I don't know where he gets it though."

I sigh. "Tiffy, please! Get to the point!"

"Oh... yeah! Anywhoo, to add insult to injury, I saw Serena here at the party, sucking up to Jonah Breck! She saw me, too. I made sure of that, you better believe it! But she's so ashamed of herself, she must be in hiding, or else she'd be in this holding pen with the rest of us."

She glances around the grand ballroom, where we're being held. Just twenty-four hours ago, she was salivating to get into this place. What a difference a day makes.

"I heard that," Emma murmurs in my ear.

"About Serena being here?" I whisper back.

"Well, yeah. But about that nut wanting me to watch her little hellion. Over my dead body! You tell her that!"

"Don't have time. I've got to get to Edwina. The sooner we put that gel on her lenses, the sooner we can figure out what's happening."

"Okay, and do me a favor: if you run into Arnie, tell him to call in." There's a quiver of fear in her voice. "I mean, protocol and all."

What she really means is that she's worried about him.

They'd make a cute couple. Maybe she's finally beginning to realize it.

I'm halfway down the hallway to Breck's office when I run into Jack. "The security detail thinks it's got its man," he tells me. "Really, it's a clown."

"Oh no, let me guess: Arnie?"

"You got it."

We both know that if they find anything on him, his cover is blown: not only for this mission, but anything else that has to do with the Quorum.

We practically run the whole way to the office.

Carl is already there, along with Arnie.

Tied to a chair.

Being slapped by one of Carl's thugs.

Half of Arnie's clown makeup has already ended up on the thug's knuckles, along with some of the blood pouring out of his nose. The thug doesn't seem too happy about this. What's left of Arnie's makeup looks like something Miro would have painted, albeit drunk on Absinthe.

"I told you I'm just another party guest!" Arnie sounds scared.

"Oh yeah?" the thug snarls at him. "The name you've given us—Lawrence Harmon—isn't on the manifest. How do you explain that?"

"I... I don't know!" Seeing us enter, Arnie closes his eyes and turns his head to the wall. He doesn't want to blow our covers.

"He's my guest." Edwina's voice comes from behind us.

Everyone turns around. She looks sickened and pale.

Carl scrutinizes her, then back at Arnie, who just sits there, silently. I can tell he's as stunned as Jack and me. "If that's the case, then why wasn't he on the manifest?"

"He was a last minute addition. He's... my date. He's been in here a million times before! Lawrence works for our florist." Slowly, she walks up to Arnie. Crouching down, she gently strokes the blood off his cheek. "My God, what have you done to him?" Stiffly, she straightens up. "Untie him immediately!"

The thug looks from her, to Carl, and back to her again. Will she super-Nanny her way around him? Obviously, she can, because he pulls loose the ties on Arnie's constraints.

Edwina nods at him, satisfied. "And I presume since, you've taken the wrong person into custody, the right one is now walking out the door with the rest of the party guests."

Carl frowns. "Who the hell told the guards to let them leave?"

Edwina hesitates, as if taken aback by the question. Finally, in a firm but menacing voice, she murmurs, "Mr. Breck did, of course. He took you at your word, that you'd caught the assassin." Defiantly, she puts her hand on Arnie's shoulder. "I'll leave it to you to tell him you were mistaken."

Carl's glare should make her wither, but she stands her ground. Really, she's holding onto Arnie. Finally, Carl snaps his fingers, Carl's thugs follow him out of the office.

Jack grabs Arnie's arm and they start out the door. When Arnie reaches the threshold, he looks back at Edwina. "I don't understand why you did it, but thank you."

She waves him on.

After they leave, I close the door behind them. Edwina flops down into a chair, burying her head in her hands.

"Why did you lie to save him?"

"Because I know he's not the shooter. He's... he's harmless."

Does she really believe that?

Whether she does or not, does it matter? Without her help, Arnie would've been killed. Forget the lens gel. Edwina may have a shady past, but I know this much: she's certainly not one of the bad guys. And at this point, that's all that matters.

"Edwina, there was a woman in the fun house with Breck. Her name is Serena, and she's Tiffy Coxhead's nanny. She's here without a green card, but Rutherford Collins solicited her for the Brecks' au pair position anyway. I saw Breck clawing at her when he got shot. But she wasn't in the grand ballroom with everyone else, and I'm concerned about her."

From the look on Edwina's face, apparently she is, too. "I—I can't take it anymore." She buries her head in her hands and sobs.

I walk over to pat her head.

The silence around us is broken by the faint buzz of her desk phone.

Slowly, as if she's carrying a hundred pounds of angst on her shoulders, she walks over to her desk and picks it up. For the longest time she says nothing. Finally, she says just two words: "Of course."

Then she hangs up.

Without another word, she opens one of the bottom drawers in her desk, and pulls out a tiny sewing kit. "I must go now. The shooting has caused the summit to be called off. In fact, Asimov has already left Lion's Lair, and Mr. Breck is on his way to the Santa Monica Airport, where he keeps his private plane. He wants to recuperate on his private island."

She plucks through a collection of buttons until she finds what she is looking for: a tiny thumb drive. She hands it to me. "Should anything happen to this Serena person—for that matter, if anything happens to me—please see that this gets to the proper authorities."

She waits for my nod, then picks up a valise and shuffles slowly out the door and down the hall, toward the elevator banks.

I, too, head out the door, toward Janie's bedroom.

I want to hug and kiss Trisha and never let her out of my sight.

But first things first: I have to get her out of this house of horrors.

CHAPTER 20

CLEANING YOUR SILVER

Tsk, tsk to tarnished flatware! It's the sign of a lazy hostess!

It's very important that you always use your very best silver for company, and that it sparkles on your table! That said, cleaning each piece prior to your party is a must. The best things to use are organic, nontoxic compounds found in every household. For example, with larger pieces, sponge on some baking soda dampened with hot water, then wipe dry with a soft cotton cloth. If the tarnish is set in deep, make a paste of the baking soda with just a little water, and leave it on the bad spots for an hour or two.

On a small piece, use toothpaste. Rub some on with your fingers and, voila, the tarnish disappears magically!

Should you want your guest to disappear with the same ease, no need to get blood on one of your newly polished knives. Just half a tablespoon of aconite does the trick. Voila, they're *dead with no mess, of what appears to be a heart attack.*

When my daughter sleeps, she looks like an angel.

I pick her up gently, and nudge her onto my shoulder. Janie, whose emotional Geiger counter is in tune with all the turmoil roiling around her, puckers her lips in protest of her best friend's desertion. "But I don't want Trisha to go home! Please let her stay, Mommy! Please?"

Babette looks helplessly at her daughter, then back to me. "I'm sorry you have to witness Janie at her worst," she murmurs. "I'm sure she's just overly tired. When she gets like this, I just don't know what to do."

"I heard you hired Serena La Costa as her new nanny. Perhaps she can help."

Babette gives me a strange look. "I hired who? Oh! The woman who was here tonight, interviewing for the position." Her hand dismisses this idea. "She left with the rest of the guests. I guess it was too much excitement for her."

"You actually saw her leave?"

"No, of course not! But she's not here, so obviously she didn't pass muster with Jonah." Babette's anger causes her cheeks to flush and eyes to narrow. "What are you implying, Donna?"

She knows what I'm asking, and why. See no evil, hear no evil, speak no evil, and you're allowed to keeping running up his credit cards without a care in the world.

I shrug in disgust. "Well then, have a safe trip."

"What do you mean? I'm not going anywhere."

"Edwina said Jonah is leaving for his private island."

A frown tamps down her usually tepid smile. "Ha! I should have known. I'm sure he's going there to lick his wounds over this whole ambassadorship debacle. That's okay. A little R&R will do him good."

"So, you aren't accompanying him?"

Her smirk curdles on her plump lips. "No. And sadly, neither is Edwina. She's been terminated. Now that he won't be accepting the ambassadorship, he has no use for her language skills and... her other special talents. Apparently, the breach in security was her fault. Asimov's people pointed this out to him. From the look on your face, I see you're disappointed. Don't worry, he'll give her a generous severance and a stellar reference—as long as she stays discreet on his behalf."

In other words, like Babette, Edwina must keep her mouth shut about Breck's twisted proclivities.

Without another word, I head out the door.

"Come here," Jack calls over to me. "You've got to see this!"

"Shhhh! Lower your voice, or you'll wake Trisha." I point to my little sleeping beauty, who is now sprawled out over the bed in our guest suite in Lion's Lair. While Jack flips through the files on the thumb drive Edwina left in my care, I'm tossing my clothes in my bag as fast as I can.

Time to get the hell outta Dodge.

Jack nods towards his iPad. "Turns out Breck sells WMDs! Not only to Asimov, but to the Afghanis, the Iranians, the Taliban, and the Quorum, too."

"Oh my God!" Without thinking, I drop the dress in my hand onto the floor. "But selling arms to known terrorists is considered treason. Wait... didn't he sell off his munitions company around the time he married Babette?"

He shakes his head in anger. "Apparently not. There's a video clip here, taken during the meeting the other night, between Breck, Asimov and Carl. Edwina must have recorded it, without Breck's knowledge. It shows that Breck still owns it—along with the Quorum. Together they set up the dummy corporation that apparently bought it."

"That way, had Breck's political career taken off as planned, no one would know of his terrorist ties," I reason. "What a great way to have your cake and eat it, too! I guess the Quorum had him over a barrel when they pushed to have Carl appointed the new CEO of his legitimate corporation, too."

"And get this. Sometimes Asimov pays him off with white slaves, which are used for another big revenue generator for Breck. He owns strip joints and whorehouses in every major city in the world! New York, London, Paris, Buenos Aries, Bangkok, you name it."

"Wait a minute: Emma told me about seeing Antoinette on a porn site—what's it called again? Oh yeah, Island of Misfit Sluts. Do you see any reference to that?"

"Hold on..." I watch as Jack slides through a few screens and taps a button or two. "There is something that sounds similar on his corporate asset sheet. Its d.b.a. is 'Misfit Quay.'"

"His private island! I'll bet it's where he takes some of the women for his own pleasure. I'm guessing he also films his smut and snuff videos there, and that his internet servers are kept on the island." I rush to the door. "Jack, Serena will end up there, too. We've got to stop him, before he takes off!"

But we can't leave Trisha here, alone."

He's right of course. "Maybe Abu is still here."

Jack punches in Abu's number. In a moment, Abu picks up. Jack quickly explains the situation then he hangs up. "Abu will be over in a moment to take Trisha home. Head out to Santa Monica airport. I'll be right behind you."

CHAPTER 21

AIRPLANE ETIQUETTE

Alas, the friendly skies have gotten downright inhospitable these days! This should not be blamed on underpaid flight attendants. Heavens knows they have enough on their hands, what with all the clueless tourists, wailing babies, and cocktail-sodden road warriors they must appease.

Your way of keeping serenity up in the air is to do the following: First, dress appropriately. Hats, gloves, stockings and your best coat will emphasize your demure disposition, albeit it means more to take off during your strip search. Next, if you're going to conceal a weapon, make sure it isn't metal, and do so in a cavity least likely to be searched. (By the way, when you figure out which one that is, let the rest of us in on this much coveted secret.)

And finally, the fact that the plane has run out of gin and vermouth is no reason to open the door and jump.

Breck's limo has a good head start, but I know a few back roads that will get me to the airport, hopefully in time.

While on the way, my cell buzzes. It's Emma. "Donna, I've finally found the intel we needed on Edwina. Believe it or not, it was in some old KGB files."

So, Babette was correct about the connection between Edwina and Asimov. "She's too young to have been an agent."

"She wasn't. But apparently, her mother, Irina Sokolov, had friends in high places. Alexei Asimov was her mother's most important lover, when he was Deputy Chairman of the KGB. His watchers kept a thorough file on him, too."

"Irina had more than one lover, and Asimov knew about it?"

"Most prostitutes do. I guess I should have called him her john. Granted she was a high-priced call girl, and had been, for at least a few years. Do they call them "call babies" if they're not yet teens? She was only fifteen when she delivered Edwina."

Just three years older than Mary. I think I'm going to throw up. "Anything else?"

"She kept it a secret from her pimp. Considering she worked the Savoy Hotel making eight hundred dollars a night, I can see why."

"Was Asimov the father?"

"Not according to the file," Emma explains. "Get a load of this. It's Jonah Breck."

The vision of Breck raping Edwina comes to mind. Does he know she is his daughter? Would he care if he did?

And Edwina referred to him as "a friend of my family's." Does she know he's more than that?

"By the way," Emma continues, "by 1990, Irina Sokolov was listed as a 'public relations executive' for one of Jonah's Moscow-based companies: the Savoy Hotel, which was the first hotel to get a gambling license."

"Which, as we all know, goes hand-in-hand with prostitution."

"Exactly. Well, one thing is for sure, she was a caring mother. She got Edwina out of Russia, and into a prestigious Swiss boarding school. Afterward, Edwina went to the Sorbonne University in Paris, where she got her Baccalaureate degree in International Business and Languages."

"Is Irina still in Russia?"

"She died. The official cause of death was a 'drug overdose,' while on vacation at some island resort. But there was also a video clip in the file of a snuff film. The woman who is getting killed looks a lot like Edwina, so I presume that is what really happened to her. Edwina was still in college at the time. How sad is that? Well, one thing for sure, Breck did Edwina a favor by firing her."

When I get to the airport, the place is empty.

The few airport personnel who are there for this midnight flight are locked in the manager's office. I hear them banging on the glass window and calling out for the police. My tingly spider senses tell me this is not a good sign. But instead of releasing them, I run past them to the gate. I'll let the cops take care of them. I've got to stop the plane from taking off, and the fewer civilians around, the better.

Great instincts, because Edwina is standing on the tarmac with Breck.

She's holding a gun to his head. Inside Breck's plane, a Gulfstream G650, the pilot is on his headset. He's obviously trying to get security to answer his frantic call for help. Rutherford Collins is also in the cockpit. He looks as if he's going to pass out, he's so pale.

As I sneak up behind her, I draw my gun but pray I don't have to use it.

"Edwina, don't shoot him! Please!"

She looks pale and weak. She flinches when I call out her name, but she doesn't drop the gun. Instead, she digs it deeper into the back of his skull. "I have to, Donna! So he doesn't hurt anyone else!"

"Jeez, it's about time someone got here and calmed this bitch down," Breck growls. "Ha! You're the last person I thought would be my savior. All this time, you've been carrying a gun? So much for Asimov's security team. So, what are you waiting for? Shoot her! Now!"

"Shut up, Breck. She's not the problem. You are." So that we understand each other, I point my gun at his crotch. "Listen, Edwina, I opened the thumb drive you gave me, and I know everything about this sadistic pig: about the munitions sales all over the world, and about the sex shops, and the porn site. I get it. He doesn't deserve to live. But if you kill him, you'll end up in jail—maybe for the rest of your life. Please, leave now, before the police get here! I'll keep him under guard until they do."

"You gave her all that information?" For a moment, Breck's anger is stronger than his fear. "Why, you cunt! You were being paid to keep your mouth shut."

Edwina does what I would have done: she shoves the gun into his mouth to shut him up. Thank goodness, because I'm tired of hearing his whiny little voice, too.

"Now that I'm here, I'll make sure he stays put until the cops come. Please, Edwina, just put down the gun and walk away now, while you still can."

"What makes you think I trust you?" Edwina's voice breaks with suspicion. "Didn't you just hear him? Your husband was willing to sacrifice you, to fatten his company's bottom line." She shakes her head in disgust. "And you were willing to go along with it, or don't you remember that? Oh, I get it, that's why you're here! He invited you to go along with him, to his magical island paradise, didn't he? You fool! Don't you know what happens on Misfit Quay? He rapes women! He ties them up, beats them, and violates them! He, and all his pals. And he puts it on the Internet. He gets away with it because he's so powerful! He did it to my mother. Then he did it to me, too!" When she stares down at him, hatred hardens her eyes. "Well, Daddy Dearest, you're not getting away this time."

"Whaw dah hawl is she tawkin' abowt?" Breck is finding it difficult to talk with Edwina's Smith & Wesson in his mouth. Should he survive this—and between her and me, the odds aren't in his favor—I'm guessing he'll include a Russian Roulette game in his sick sex itinerary.

"I do know what he does there! Edwina, between his sex slavery business and his illegal munitions sales, he's looking at jail time for life—if they don't fry him as a traitor."

She smiles at the thought. "Ha! That would be sweet. It would have been simpler than setting up the hits on him."

"You mean, the assassins were after Breck, not Asimov?"

Edwina nods. "Wherever Asimov would be standing, Jonah would be right beside him. It would have looked like an accident. As if they'd shot the wrong man. At least I paid them with funds I funneled from his off-shore bank accounts!"

"You bitch!" Breck yells. "You embezzled... from me?"

She nods proudly. "That's okay. Where you're going, you won't need money."

Ah, now so much makes sense. "It was you who shot Breck in the House of Mirrors, wasn't it?"

Edwina nods. "When the assassins missed the hit, I realized I had to do it myself. I tried to poison him. I'd coated the champagne glasses with cyanide, but Asimov's consultant made the butler drink from one first." She frowns. "And it was you who shot me in the House of Mirrors, wasn't it?"

I realize now why she's so pale. It is from the loss of blood. "Yes. But now, knowing what I do, I wish I hadn't. "

"Not me. I wished I'd died back there." Her voice is so low, I can barely hear her. "They should fry him, along with all the others in their private little club, that 'Quorum.'

Breck is a member of the Quorum?

Now things make sense: his closeness to Asimov, as well as some of the Third World dictators, all of who we now know are his munitions customers.

As much as I'd like to see a bullet in his head, his rendition would give us so much we need to know to take the Quorum down.

I can't let her shoot him.

And besides, if Edwina is to escape, it's now or never. "Edwina, I'll make sure he pays for his crimes, to all those women, including your mother. I know he raped her when she was only fifteen. I know she saved you from the same living hell he put her through."

My declaration takes her off guard. Her wrist relaxes around the gun.

And that's all Breck needs to make his move.

He slaps Edwina's gun from her hand, but it falls too far away for him to go for it.

While she scrambles for the gun, he elbows me in the gut. I double over, but I won't let go of my gun. That doesn't stop him from making a grab for it. As we wrestle with it, she stands there, helpless and stunned. She doesn't want to shoot me, or miss him.

Not Breck. He knows exactly what he is doing. When he bends my arm so that the gun is pointed directly at her, he squeezes my trigger finger, without a second thought.

The bullet hits her straight through the heart.

She staggers back, then drops to the ground, up against the

wheels of the plane. But her eyes stare out at him until her life ebbs from her, along with all the hate and pain and sadness that has made it a living hell.

"You son of a bitch! That was Irina Sokolov's daughter."

"No shit?" He stops to contemplate that. "Now that you mention it, there was a resemblance."

"You dirty son of a bitch! Don't you get it? Edwina was your daughter!"

"She's my... what?" He shakes his head, hard and long. "Bullshit! That's a lie." He turns toward the plane. "You're one sick bitch—which, sadly, is my type. So if you want to hop onboard—"

That's it.

My first shot slams into the tarmac, at his feet. That was just for fun, to watch him dance a jig and squeal like the revolting little piggy he is.

I'm having so much fun that I don't hear the Los Angeles SWAT team runnin' and gunnin' around me until the team leader yells, "Police! Drop your weapon and on the floor, spread eagle! Now!"

Here goes a great pair of Michael Kors slacks. But I do as I am told, and pray Jack gets here, pronto, to clear the air, so to speak.

In the meantime, Breck howls, "Thank God you're here, officers. I'm Jonah Breck. This—this lunatic killed my assistant, and was about to kill me, too! She jealous and mad because I won't leave my wife for her!"

I can't believe this clown. He thinks I'm going to take the rap for him? "He's lying, officer. He's the one who killed her, not me!"

The SWAT leader looks at Breck, then to me, and back to Breck. "Oh yeah? The shot came from her gun! Take it and test it. My fingerprints are nowhere around it. My poor secretary was just trying to protect herself from this jealous nut. I'm on my way to Washington D.C., right now, to meet with the president. I'm to be the new ambassador to Russia."

"I can confirm that, officers!" Rutherford says waving a white flag out the door. "Feel free to look at our flight plan."

The officer hesitates, then nods.

"Officer, you can't let them go! He's a traitor! He sells arms to terrorists. Not only that, but he keeps sex slaves on his private island!"

"See? What did I say? This woman is as nutty as she sounds." As Breck passes me, he murmurs, "Spread-eagle is a great look for you, Donna."

I grab his ankle and he falls onto his knees. But before I can jump him, I've got a SWAT-regulation boot on the center of my spine, pushing me back down onto the asphalt.

My face is crammed sideways, but in the direction I'm facing I can see Breck stumble up the ramp. The plane door slams shut behind him, and a moment later, the plane taxis down the runway and leaves the ground. I can see it again as it banks back over the airport and out toward the sea.

The next thing I know, I'm being lifted onto my feet and read my Miranda rights. My hands are pushed behind my back, and I'm handcuffed. A police car is driven onto the tarmac, and I'm shoved into the back of the squad car.

It drives off the runway. When we hit the gate outside the

airport, six other Santa Monica PD black-and-whites fall into line behind us.

As we turn down Arizona Avenue, Jack's Lamborghini speeds past us. I'm sure every cop in my entourage is jonesing to chase after him. No need. He does a U-turn in the middle of the street in order to flip around and follow us back to the station.

Hopefully, he'll be able to get me out of this jam, as soon as possible. I miss my children, my home, and my bed.

I miss feeling Jack's arms around me.

I can't help but wonder if Acme will consider our mission a success or a failure, considering all the assassins were exterminated despite the fact that they weren't after the target we'd presumed.

Oh yeah, and the summit was cancelled before it started.

On a classroom scale, my guess is that we earned a C+.

Okay, maybe a D.

We should at least get an A for effort.

CHAPTER 22

SAYING GOOD-BYE TO YOUR HOSTESS

Inevitably, the party has to come to an end.

Under ideal circumstances, this is not when (a) the place is on fire; (b) the joint is being raided; or (c) when a murder most foul has been committed. (Admittedly, any of these incidents would put a damper on an otherwise successful soirée.)

When you feel it is time to leave (or that you've worn out your welcome), hopefully, it won't be after everyone else has already gone. Heaven forbid you should be that last annoyingly longwinded   can't-take-a-hint-no-matter-how-much-she-yawns guest!

And you certainly cannot slip out in the shank of the evening, without even a simple fare-the-well. (Unless you've pilfered through her jewelry box and helped yourself to that strand of her grandmother's pearls you've always admired. Then certainly, run like hell.)

In the same token, make sure you aren't the first to walk out the door. This relays the unspoken message that you find her party deadly dull. (Even if that is the case, you would hate for her to think so, especially when you could have taken it upon yourself to liven things up by spicing the punch with a tab or two of LSD).

My cell in the Santa Monica hoosegow could do with a little sprucing up, but my roomies, Big Bitch Bitsy and Shitfaced Leona, would get in my face and threaten me with some smackdown should I even consider rearranging their fine collection of Chippendales trading cards, which has been stuck onto the concrete wall with Bubblicious.

I've been in this hellhole for the past seven hours. I don't plan on staying here another night. Still, Bitsy (whereas she uses this as a surname, I don't want to disrespect her by calling her by the much less bestie-friendly Big or Bitch) is no fool. She sees me eyeing the bottom bunk near the window, and wants to set me straight up front that it's hers. Bitsy's fist goes for my nose. To her surprise, I'm able to stop it with my stiffened palm, and twist her arm out behind her, which is all it takes to warn her that not only sticks and stones, but pressure in the right spot, is all it takes to break her bones. Being raised by gentlefolk, I release her with a warning that doesn't mar the reputation of the woman who bore her, or reference some embarrassing part of her anatomy.

You'd think she'd take the hint that I'm not someone she should be messing with, but no.

The long shadows cast by our cell's fugly fluorescent overhead light tip me off that she's about to stab me with a shiv made from a metal spring from Leona's bunk. A roundhouse kick to Bitsy's gut sends her reeling backward into the wall. I cram her head against it with my version of a Vulcan Mind Meld, where pressure points in three key spots on her cranium has Bitsy repeating every word I say. "I will act like a lady at all times. I will share with my bunkmates. I will talk in a lady-like voice. I won't use my nasty pottymouth."

Works every time. Thank you, Mr. Spock.

"Tsk, tsk. Is that any way to make friends and influence enemies?"

I turn around to find Jack smiling at me from just beyond the bars. So, that was the reason for the salacious whistles and catcalls coming from the other cells. Usually, it's for a new prisoner, or as they call them here, "fresh meat." This time it's for six-feet-two-inches of prime beefcake in an Armani suit.

I wave gaily at him. Okay, it's more like a middle-finger salute. "'Bout damn time you got here. If it's going to take you seven hours to drive a whole two miles, why do you own a Lamborghini?"

"Because the girls love it." Noting my raised brow and Bitsy's shiv in my hand has him rethinking his answer. "In all seriousness, Ryan and I are having a hell of a time convincing the local authorities that you didn't kill Edwina. It doesn't help that your prints are the only ones on the murder weapon."

"But I explained that to the SWAT guys! It was in my hand when Breck and I wrestled for it, and he twisted my arm so that it was pointing at her when he squeezed the trigger."

"Likely story," mutters Leona, through her drunken stupor.

I peel her favorite Chippendale off the wall and tear it in half. She whimpers, but takes the hint that she better keep mum in front of my gentleman caller.

Jack shakes his head at my cruelty. "It doesn't help that the security video shows you as coming out of the House of Mirrors right after Breck got shot in there."

Suddenly, it looks like I'll have the time to complete a full makeover of my jail cell.

I smack the bars between us with my fist. "Oh my God! If I end up in jail for Edwina's murder, Carl will be given custody of the kids! I've got to get out of this mess!"

"Don't worry about Carl. The files Edwina left behind have put him back on the Watch List, and Breck, too for that matter. Unfortunately, Carl left with Asimov's contingent before we could stop him."

"Well, that's some relief." I feel tears forming in my eyes. "What have you told the children about my absence?"

"Just that you were in the wrong place at the wrong time. Unfortunately, your arrest made the news in a big way. The police leaked Breck's version of it. Needless to say, all of Hilldale is buzzing about it. Penelope and her posse actually believe that you're jealous of Babette. Mrs. Breck's silence on the topic isn't helping matters."

"Figures she'd be toeing his party line." I shake my head in disgust. "Breck is a member of the Quorum. For that alone, we've got to bring him back. Seriously, Jack, what are we going to do?"

"We just have to wait it out, for however long it takes." He looks down at his watch "Which should be about... now."

For just a few seconds, all the lights in the jail flash.

Jack looks down the hall. Seeing that the two guards have been distracted by the shouts of the cellmates over this disruption of their routine, he slips me a small bag through the bars.

"That was Arnie," he mutters, just barely loud enough for me to hear. "He's just put their security feed on a loop. It'll run for a couple of hours. In the meantime, this spray turns these two into sleeping beauties. If need be, you can use the spray on the guards, too, but I think the diversion Arnie is causing in Cell Block C will keep them busy for awhile. We guessed at the uniform size. The smart card gets you through every door in this joint. Abu and I will be waiting down the block in his ice cream truck."

I give him a thumbs up. I wish I could kiss him, but I don't want to make my roomies jealous.

I'm just glad he's kept his shirt on, and he's kept his bowtie and French cuffs at home.

CHAPTER 23

HOW TO HAVE A BEACH'ING PAR-TAY!

An outdoor party is always a welcomed change of pace! Forego the backyard barbecue for something a little more adventurous, like a clambake at the beach.

Set your coals in the sand and fire them up. When they're white-hot, they're ready for a galvanized tub lined with seaweed. Fill with two pounds of clams, a half a dozen pounds of small red potatoes, some white wine, and a dozen ears of corn wrapped in tin foil. Cover the tub with wet burlap, and keep the top wet so that the food steams up nice, and you'll have quite a feast!

Afterwards, any out-of-line guests can do a walk of shame— over the hot coals, of course.

Misfit Quay is the smallest gem on the necklace of islands, which make up Turks and Caicos. It is also the one farthest south and west: so close to our government's Guantánamo Bay Detention Camp, on Cuba. I've no doubt the prisoners there could see it, if their cells had windows.

If Gitmo's tortures were seen online, I wonder if the number of Internet hits would be as high as those for the Island of Misfit Sluts.

My guess is that it would come close.

We're just a half mile off Misfit Quay's south shore, in a three-man submarine. From here, we can easily see that what Breck calls his "sand castle" is really a full-blown palatial retreat.

From Acme's fixed-position satellite, we can monitor everyone on the property who shows up as infrared hot spots: the sixteen guards on their surveillance wall posts and all entries and exits, and another six warm bodies inside its various control rooms.

The master bedroom is easy to find. It's on the very top floor of the retreat. Its large terrace has a straight-on view of the splendid tropical sunsets.

We detect the auras of three hotspots inside the room. One can be seen spread-eagled against a wall. Another image can be made out, curled against a bench. Their torturer moves between them. When he strikes with the instrument in his hand, they flinch.

I can only imagine their screams.

I force my gaze from this scrim of terror in order to scrutinize it for our entry point. Finally I spot some sort of pipe, which runs under the retreat's main building. Every fifteen minutes or so—perhaps it's sewage, or maybe runoff from the property's numerous freshwater ponds and pool—cascades from it, creating a waterfall against a two-story wall of natural rocks.

I point it out to Jack.

"Yep, that's our way in," he murmurs.

We leave the submarine anchored in a thatch of mangroves around a hundred feet from this manmade falls, then grope our way up the rocky slope until we reach the water pipe.

When the flow seems to trickle to a stop, Jack nods to me. "Ladies first."

That is such a fucked-up notion in so many ways. Climbing a wet rock wall is one of them.

There are only two guards between Breck and us, both on the floor below his bedroom penthouse suite.

They go down without knowing what hit them: a bullet through the heart.

What we haven't counted on is that the elevator doors open into the center of the room. Granted, they do so with a slight whooshing sound, then close just as quickly.

The only thing that keeps Breck from looking up is that he's having too much fun fucking one of his captives on her hands and knees, doggie style. It is Antoinette. When she moans, he twists the harness in her mouth so that her neck snaps back, causing her to cry out even louder.

"What took you so long?" Breck says.

Jack and I look at each other. Apparently, Breck is expecting someone else. The more the merrier would be typical of Breck's perverted sexual appetite.

We better move quickly.

Jack motions me to stand directly behind Breck. I nod and move into position, training my gun on the back of his head while Jack sidles up behind the girl strapped to the wall which curves just beyond the elevator circular bank. It is Serena. She's sobbing, and her back is stripped to a bloody pulp. He touches her gently, on her bicep. When she looks up, he puts a finger to his lips as he unties one wrist tether, then the other, before loosening the straps around her ankles. He then gives me the high sign before stepping back behind the rounded elevator shaft, and out of sight.

I nod back, then shout, "Get off of her, Breck."

Breck turns around. When he sees me, the color leaves his face. "What the hell?"

"I said get off of her."

I hate the way he smiles at me, as if I'm joking. To prove I'm not, I shoot at his foot, missing it deliberately.

Yep, he gets the point now. He raises his hands and rises slowly.

If only I could knock that shit-eating grin off his face.

He glances at the elevator. Then back to me again. "Finally! Now, do what you should have done back at Lion's Lair and kill this bitch."

I turn toward the elevator to find Carl standing there.

I'm sure I look as if I've seen a ghost.

"Sorry, hon, but he's got a point. You can be such a bitch." He cocks his gun and pulls the trigger. His head tilts toward me, as if a nod of sympathy makes up for five and half years of living hell.

It can't. But the bullet that slams into Breck's forehead is a step in the right direction.

Then I remember that I needed Breck to ruin Carl. Yeah, that wipes the smile off my face, and fast.

"What the hell are you doing here?...And what the hell did you do that for?"

"Just cleaning house. Once I heard Edwina gave you a memory drive with all those files, I knew this would be your next stop. Breck was such a pussy. He'd have turned Witness Protection after an hour of jail time." He looks around the corner, where Jack and Serena stand—

Stood. They're gone now.

Carl's next bullet is for Antoinette. It hits her squarely between the eyes. She dies with a gasp, collapsing onto the bed. Her dead eyes stare up at me.

"Damn you, Carl! You had to kill her, too?"

"Collateral damage. You know how the game's played."

"Yeah, I know." I kneel beside Antoinette. Gently I close her eyes. Then I stand and turn to him. "Am I going to be collateral damage, too?"

He tilts his head in sympathy. "Like I said, you know how the game is played."

"How could you? I'm the mother of your children!"

"An inconvenient truth. You're also standing between me and full custody of my little darlings."

"I'm willing to share joint custody." I smile hopefully when I say this.

"Sorry, but I'm not." He points his gun at my head.

Even the waves crashing on the rocks below seem to go silent at the sound of Jack cocking the trigger of his gun.

Carl turns fast, but he's too late. Jack's bullet bores a hole black and deep into his shoulder that turns candy apple red within seconds.

Carl drops his gun as he staggers onto Breck's torture bench.

Jack picks it up and hands it to me. "Here's your chance to get him out of your life, once and for all."

He's right. I now have the chance to kill one of America's Most Wanted, and number twelve on the Interpol Watch List.

Who also just happens to be the father of my children.

And let's not forget he just had a gun pointed at my head.

Oh yes, and just the other day, he threw me off a restaurant's patio ledge, into the Pacific Ocean.

Not to mention the bullet he put into me just a few months ago.

No doubt about it, one shot to the heart would certainly be quicker than a divorce.

"I wish I could say I'm sorry, Carl, but here's the thing: I'm just not that into you anymore." I take aim. My finger leans on the trigger ever so gently.

"Donna, I know this won't change anything between you and me, but I'd be remiss if I didn't mention it."

"Carl, our kids have a heavy carpool schedule. From what I can see, the three parents they still have are all in this room, which leaves them in the care of an aunt with cataracts, a bad heart, and a driving record that would earn her the inside track in a demolition derby, so get to the point."

"Okay, sure: I'll make it snappy. Even if we do divorce, you know this guy won't marry you, right?"

Here it comes, the jealousy. My sigh is loud and tired. "That's between him and me, Carl. But if you want to waste your last breath casting aspersions on Jack, then by all means, go for it. Why won't he marry me?"

Carl smiles over at Jack. "Because he's already got a wife."

Suddenly I feel faint.

Carl is just messing with me. He wants me to drop the gun. But no, instead I lower it from his heart to his cock.

"Is he bullshitting me?" I don't need to see Jack's face to gauge the truth in his voice, to listen to his words of reassurance.

But, hell yeah, I need him to reassure me. Like, now.

So, why isn't he saying anything?

"He's... he's right." Jack's voice comes out in a dead mutter. "I'm married."

Ah. Well.

Now he tells me?

I should've known better. I should've read between the lines. All that malarkey about the need to wait for him to "sort things out" wasn't ambivalence. It was his way of saying I'm not available.

And yes, I know better: I'm not supposed to take my eyes off my target, let alone allow my hands to shake.

Or drop my arm to my side.

This is all Carl needs to make his move. He kicks Jack in the gut, then follows up with an elbow to the nose. As Jack doubles over, Carl smirks. "You'll never take my place."

Then he leaps into the elevator and pushes the button.

For a last fleeting moment, we share a stare. But Carl's triumphant smile is undercut by the pity in his eyes. No doubt my own face resembles a Picasso puzzle, distended and distorted by the jagged emotions of hurt and anger and shame.

I fall to the floor and bury my head in my hands.

When, finally, the wind fills Jacks lungs again, he rasps out, "Donna, you have to believe me! I was just waiting for the right time to tell you."

I struggle up onto my feet and head for the elevator. When I pass him, I drop his gun on the floor beside him, but keep walking. "When you get home, pack your things. You're moving out."

Serena, who has been hiding behind the elevator shaft, slips in after me.

She shakes off her terror and pats my shoulder gently, all the way down to the ground floor.

Chapter 24

Funeral Attire

Everyone knows black is the appropriate color to wear to a funeral. That said, it is not the occasion to wear your favorite little black dress. However, demure couture will make a statement, as opposed to a plunging neckline, going backless, or with a skirt too tight or too short.

A chapeau is a nice touch. Stay away from chef's hats or baseball caps, even if the cap you choose bears the logo of the deceased's favorite sports team. It's just not good form.

By the way, if it's an open coffin, resist the urge to play "Spot the Bullet Holes" with the corpse. If the family used a good mortician, he will have done a pretty decent plug and patch job, so don't ruin the illusion for the rest of the bereaved.

Breck's funeral is well attended by his political cronies and every titan of industry.

But what has the crowd abuzz isn't all these famous faces. It's the sight of me standing beside Babette, who has her arm entwined in mine.

The official cause of death is a heart attack. Minus the mortician's handiwork, that would have seemed rather suspect.

Thanks to Babette, the criminal charges against me have been dropped. It's her way of paying me back for keeping mum about the fact that her husband was the biggest traitor this country has ever known. The truth would ruin her reputation and Janie's young life.

Jack and Abu are here, too. So are Emma and Arnie, but they are watching from a distance, providing surveillance of the crowd. The video will be analyzed later today. Now that we have proof Breck was one of the Quorum, we presume other members are in the crowd.

Not Carl. That would be downright crass.

Serena isn't there, either. She took advantage of Misfit Quay's close proximity to her homeland of Venezuela and requested that our helicopter drop her there. I can't blame her. Her country may have a Loony Tune dictator, but she'd rather take her chances there with him, than over here, in the company of a bunch of sick corporate fucks and desperate housewives.

It looks like our mission has been rated a surprising B+. True, the summit's failure gave POTUS a very public black eye. On the other hand, Edwina's digital files have been invaluable in tracking down despots with errant WMDs. It also gives POTUS leverage over Asimov. The last thing the new Russian president needs is a revolt on his hands for selling his country's women as sex slaves.

Ryan has refused my request to "divorce" Jack.

"It's his cover," he says. "You'll have to learn to live with it."

Even when I begged, he wouldn't budge. Instead, he gave me a rotten impersonation of JFK. "Ask not what your country can do for you, but what you can do for—"

At that point, I walked out, slamming the door behind me. Everyone thinks they can pull off a Kennedy accent. Here's a news bulletin. You can't do Kennedy. You can't do Elvis, either. Live with it.

So Jack now sleeps in the guest room. I don't know if that will cure his amnesia, and I know it won't heal my broken heart. But what else can I do?

This is exactly the question I ask my shrink, Dr. Hartley.

Of course he's confused by it. "Wait...I thought your goal was to divorce him."

"I'm divorcing the deserter. The papers were served, and everything. The guy I'm talking about now is his... replacement."

"Oh." Dr. Bob tilts his head back as he considers this new bit of information. "Okay, well, you certainly moved fast. And replacement is... well, it's a tough word to use in a relationship."

"Your advice was to get on with my life, so I did."

He smiles, pleased that I took his sage words to heart. "You're right. Let's not get hung up on semantics. So, what's the issue with the new man in your life?"

"Apparently he's married to someone else. That little tidbit conveniently slipped his mind. I feel as if I'm in a bad dream."

"Been there, done that." Dr. Bob laughs tepidly. "Donna, it all boils down to this. You love him, but you no longer trust him."

I nod. He's hit the nail on the head.

"Can you think of a reason why he wouldn't have told you this information up front?"

"Other than the fact I might have killed him? Hmmm. Well, let's see. We met because we work together. We didn't like each other initially, so I never bothered to ask. When things heated up between us, he never offered it, because they're separated."

"Now that you know, have you given him a chance to explain himself fully?"

"Not really. We've just come back from a business trip. Between that and the kids—"

"No excuses. If you feel the relationship is worth salvaging, you two need to talk. You need to hear him out. It's time both of you put your cards on the table. Otherwise, you'll never be able to trust him, and it will be over anyway." He leans in. "Donna, if you don't resolve it with him, you may never trust anyone, ever again."

He's right, and I know it.

"Okay, Doc. Thanks." I smile through my tears. "You wife is a very lucky woman, to be married to such an insightful man. What's her name again?"

"Joanna... I mean, Emily!" He shakes his head at the slip up. "See? Easy to do. Just give him a chance to make things right."

When I enter the Sand Dollar, Anna's brow raises in concern. "I'm almost afraid to ask. Your usual table?"

I nod. "And Jack is meeting me here."

"Good. The other dude needs an anger management course, big time."

"Or a long plane ride around the world, where the flight attendants make him wear a hood while they're waterboarding him."

She shrugs. "I've dated a few who deserve a ticket on that airline." She grabs a couple of menus. "Follow me."

My date doesn't keep me waiting long. He's got a dozen yellow roses, my favorite.

We give Anna the high sign for our usual. After she brings us our drinks, Jack takes a gulp, then clears his throat. "You're right. The moment we knew this relationship was what we both wanted, I should have told you everything."

I nod, but say nothing.

"Her name is Valentina Petrescu."

"The name is, what, Polish?"

"Romanian. She was a gymnast."

A gymnast? Figures.

"You may recognize her. She was on the Olympic team that won the gold, twelve, thirteen years ago." He takes a photo out of his pocket. The woman in it can't be more than nineteen or twenty, at the most. She's doing a flip off the double parallel bars.

"She seems quite... flexible."

He can't stifle the smile on his lips. "Yeah... well, she was flexible, in another way. Her father, a university professor, had been falsely accused of being a dissident. To get him out of prison, she approached the SIE—Romania's Foreign Intelligence arm—to become a carrier. As a gymnast, she had the perfect cover."

"How were you able to turn her?"

"You mean, other than my obvious charms?"

Seeing that I'm not laughing, he shrugs.

"They did it for me when they killed her father. And not by throwing him back in jail. He was so ashamed of the position he'd put her in that he sliced his wrists in the bathtub. She found him after coming home from a tournament in Germany."

I can see the pain in his eyes—pain he feels for her. It is enough to make me look away.

"So, she got word to our side that she was willing to double up?"

"Yes. I was working that part of the world and was assigned to be her handler for a while. We became... close."

"What happened to your 'happily ever after?'"

"Someone tipped off the SIE. They put a tail on her while she was at the European Gymnastics Championships in Paris, and she was caught making a drop. She escaped to one of our safe houses. To keep her from being sent back to Romania, I married her. This gave her diplomatic immunity."

"Then I take it, yours was a marriage of convenience."

"I'd be lying if I said I wasn't in love with her. We're beyond lying to each other, aren't we, Donna?"

"I hope so." I wipe away a tear. "Which begs the question, why aren't you with her now?"

His back stiffens. "She was in love with someone else. End of story."

"Obviously not, or else you wouldn't still be married to her."

He looks around, at the other couples seated around us, all of whom are laughing, smiling, or holding hands.

We could be like that, if he loved me instead of her.

He gives his head a single angry shake. "In hindsight, I should have killed him. I've survived her duplicity, but Acme is still playing catch-up."

"I... I don't get it. She fell in love with another agent?"

He doesn't answer me.

He doesn't have to. His gaze is weighted with compassion. Or is that commiseration? And if so, why?

Then it hits me. "Carl."

He nods. "I thought she'd be happy to retire. She was, at first. We had a little place in Paris in the Fourth Arrondissement, on the Île de la Cité. They met there. It was a stupid thing to do, but I brought him home with me because he thought his hotel room had been compromised. That night we let off steam. We drank and told old war stories. He was charming. She was fascinated. Little did I know she was also bored. A bored housewife."

Yes, Carl can be charming. It's how he gets away with murder.

"Sometimes he came to town when I was on assignment."

Before I can ask the question, he adds quickly, "And no, I don't know when it started up between them. For years now, I've been trying to figure out the whole timeline. Was he already a Quorum operative when I first brought him home? In hindsight, Ryan seemed to think so. Did he seduce my wife in order to search our apartment for intel? The day she left, a microdot with the code to access the DasS cloud with the Acme Directory went with her."

"Oh my God." I shake my head in dismay. This digital directory, which lives on a virtual private network, lists every agent, and every mission, as well as all our leads, assets, agents, and contacts in nations and agencies around the world.

"Of course, at first I didn't suspect either of them. I'd been away for a week. When I got home, I found a note that said, 'I'll be home soon.' She added something that, at the time, I thought was a joke. 'Jusqu'à ce que la mort nous sépare.' In English, it means, 'Until death do us part.'"

"The wedding vow?"

"Yes."

"Why did you consider it a joke?"

"I guess 'joke' is the wrong word. We gave our vows in front of a civil judge. At the time, Valentina knew very little French, but the judge insisted she repeat the vow in his language, word for word. Afterward, we laughed at this." He puts down his drink. "When I first read the phrase in the note she left behind, I presumed it was her way of kidding around. You know, a sweet way of saying she missed me. But when I realized the microdot was missing, and she never came back that night, I presumed she'd taken it with her, perhaps as leverage in case the SIE caught up with her. For the longest time I had faith that, one day, she'd come home to me. Still, you can imagine what Ryan's reaction was when I broke the news to him."

"Ha! I'm glad I wasn't part of Acme then."

"You came on the scene a year or so later. Carl's supposed murder was reported a week or two after Valentina's disappearance. I didn't put two and two together until eighteen months ago, when I saw video of a hit that went down in Bulgaria. The assassins took out an Acme agent who was following up on some chatter regarding a Quorum mission. As luck would have it, the hit was caught on a surveillance camera. The shooter was a woman. Valentina."

"What a transition!"

He nods. "We all have it in us, I guess, when we're angry enough. You're a perfect example of that. I got angry, too, when Carl was ID'ed at the murder scene. He was driving the getaway car. That was when we realized he'd faked his own death."

Jack is right. Anger changes us. Right now, I should be feeling angry at Jack. But I now find it hard to be, knowing that he and I have something else in common: spouses who betrayed us.

Their betrayal made us different people, too.

Sadder people.

I'm through letting Carl ruin my life. I don't know if Jack feels the same way about Valentina. Only time will tell. In the meantime, I can only hope and pray that, in time, we can both put our past behind us and realize a future together.

I pick up his hand and kiss it gently. "Let's go home."

"You don't want to order something?" He strokes my cheek

gently, as if I'm some apparition who might disappear again into that darker dimension from which I've just emerged.

I pick up his bouquet and breathe deeply into its fragrant petals. "Nope. It's time to stop and smell the roses. I'm guessing they'll smell even better floating in our bathroom Jacuzzi tub. Care to join me?"

He doesn't have to be asked twice. He tosses some cash on the table for our drinks, then takes my hand and pulls me through the restaurant, toward the lobby and out the door.

There's something about makeup sex that makes it so special. Perhaps it's the urgency you feel to get beyond "I'm so pissed at you" to "I'm so horny for you" that makes it hard to keep your hands off each other's bodies. Or maybe it's the way your skin tingles whenever his finger grazes your skin, or when his tongue tickles your nipple.

During makeup sex, have you ever noticed that, when your hand wraps around his cock, it instantly springs up, grows large, and stays stiff? It beckons to you. The slit in the head is like a sly wink, and the gentle curve of the shaft gives a nod as if to say, "I missed you! I can't live without you! Hurry up and climb onboard! Don't worry! I'll make you happy."

Content. Satisfied. Lusted after.

Loved.

Jack doesn't wait until the tub is filled before pulling me down into the churning bubbles with him. The water is warm and yet I shiver, not because I'm cold, but from the anticipation that is stoked by his soft gaze of adoration. By his hot, deep kisses. By the way his hand slowly caresses my mound before his long, thick fingers slip between its lips. Gently and methodically, he synchronizes his strokes to the natural rhythm of my desire.

As I burst, I bury my head in the pulsing water. My scream ripples up. When I resurface, he's laughing. "You sound like a mermaid."

"Oh yeah? Well, a mermaid can't do this." I straddle him, pulling his knees tightly around me. As I rock up and down on his cock, I only get tighter. The way his eyes widen shows me he loves what he is feeling.

His orgasm propels me up out of the warm water and into the cold air, where my nipples harden. He doesn't mind this at all. In fact, he places his hands on them. This warms them up again.

Then he buries his head between my breasts for so long that I assume he's fallen asleep.

But no. He's smiling when, finally, he looks up at me. "Let's fight every day."

My response is to pull his legs out from under him, so that he drops under the water.

I think he gets the message because he pulls me under, too.

We're still entwined in each other's arms when we're

awakened by a steady tapping on our bedroom door, which gets more frantic with each passing moment, as do Trisha's plaintive whispers, "Mommy! Daddy! Open up!"

Jack can groan all he wants, but she isn't going away.

I reach for my robe, and toss the bedspread over Jack. He takes this as my tacit approval that he can go back to sleep.

I try to look stern as I peek out the door, but it's hard to be cross with a five-year-old pirouetting in a pink tutu. With one leg outstretched, she hops toward me on the other. Then with all the grace of the dearly departed Black Swan, she hands me an envelope embellished with a lipstick heart.

"It's for Daddy," she whispers.

"Trisha, how many times do I have to tell you my lipsticks aren't crayons?"

Her mouth purses into a pout. "I didn't decorate the envelope, Mommy! The lady gave it to me that way."

"A lady? Who is she?" I look down the stairwell. Thank goodness the front door is closed.

"None of those ladies you don't like. This one was pretty. Mommy, is it Valentine's Day?"

"No, sweetie, but it will soon be Halloween." I stare down at envelope, then over at Jack. Yes, I'm tempted to open it.

I shake off this urge. My resolve is now aimed at my daughter. "Lock the front door. You know the rules. Next time, ask Mary to open it."

"I did! But she wouldn't get off the phone." Miffed that I'm shooting the messenger, she twirls around three times before hop scotching down the stairs.

I close the door with a click. Jack has the pillow over his head, so he can't hear it. Nor can he see me as I slide a nail under the gummed flap of the envelope and nudge it open, gently...slowly...

The handwritten card has no signature, and just one line:

Jusqu'à ce que la mort nous sépare.

Until death do us part.

To keep from sobbing, I seek pain somewhere other than my heart by piercing my palm with the same nail that opened the envelope.

I had hoped he'd stay asleep until my tears stopped, but no. Instinctively he reaches over for me. Finding the bed empty beside him, he rolls over and opens one eye.

I don't have to tell him something is wrong. He can read it in my face.

I walk over and hand him the envelope. The blood red heart on the outside tells him all he needs to know. Still, he pulls out the note that confirms it, then looks over at me in disbelief.

No need to beat around the bush. Even if he won't say it, I will.

"Honey, she's home."

He slides back down in the bed.

I do, too.

We lay back to back.

"She's a problem we're going to have to deal with." I say this so softly I'm not certain he hears me.

Until he responds, "So is Carl."

We turn and hold each other.

OTHER NOVELS BY JOSIE BROWN

THE TRUE HOLLYWOOD LIES SERIES

Hollywood Hunk

Hollywood Whore

Hollywood Heiress
Release Date: 2016

THE TOTLANDIA SERIES

The Onesies - Book 1 (Fall)

The Onesies - Book 2 (Winter)

The Onesies - Book 3 (Spring)

The Onesies - Book 4 (Summer)

The Twosies - Book 5 (Fall)

The Twosies - Book 6 (Winter)
Release Date: Winter 2016

MORE JOSIE BROWN NOVELS

The Candidate

Secret Lives of Husbands and Wives

The Baby Planner

CPSIA information can be obtained
at www.ICGtesting.com
Printed in the USA
LVOW04s1742040816
499079LV00022B/711/P